Nayantara Sahgal is the author of several works of fiction and non-fiction, the first of which, *Prison and Chocolate Cake*, an autobiography, was published in 1954. Her works include classic novels such as *Rich Like Us, Plans for Departure* and *Lesser Breeds*. She has received the Sahitya Akademi Award, the Sinclair Prize and the Commonwealth Writers' Prize. Her novel, *When the Moon Shines by Day*, was longlisted for the 2018 JCB Prize. She returned her Akademi Award in 2015 in protest against the murder by vigilantes of three writers, and the Akademi's silence at the time. She has been a Vice President of the PUCL (People's Union for Civil Liberties) and is engaged in an ongoing protest against the assaults on the freedom of expression and democratic rights.

PRAISE FOR *WHEN THE MOON SHINES BY DAY*

'A vital, timely, thought-provoking and deeply relevant work of writing.' —Kankana Basu in the *Asian Age*

'Sahgal packs a punch in this political fiction which has an almost eerie touch of reality in the current backdrop ... The strands of reality and fiction are so well intertwined and woven that one gets the whiff of the familiar even in the most bizarre situations painted by the writer. This shows the skill of Sahgal as a writer.' —*The Tribune*

'The power of [*When the Moon Shines by Day*] also lies in exposing personages and events of history in a manner that is enlightening without being too didactic ... It reflects the disturbingly divisive discourse and organized violence that pervades our milieu, making it an example of "factual" fiction.' —*The Telegraph*

PRAISE FOR *THE FATE OF BUTTERFLIES*

'In writing this novella at this time, [Sahgal] is not only discharging her responsibility as a writer but also calling on artists, dancers and connoisseurs to shore fragments of culture "against our ruins"... Form and substance meld in the timely message of the book.' —Anuradha Marwah in *Biblio*

'Sahgal is a vital writer, her refusal to kowtow an example that should shame many of our institutions, not least our media.' —Shougat Dasgupta in *India Today*

'Before one has realised it, *The Fate of Butterflies* ... has captured you. It has got you in the claws of the human monsters it describes, in the jaws of the human beasts it portrays. It has disturbed you in a way that you cannot ever get over the "disturbance".' —Gopalkrishna Gandhy in *Scroll.in*

The Unmaking of India Chronicles

When the Moon Shines by Day

and

The Fate of Butterflies

TWO NOVELS

Nayantara Sahgal

SPEAKING TIGER

SPEAKING TIGER BOOKS LLP
125A, Ground Floor, Shahpur Jat, near Asiad Village,
New Delhi 110049

When the Moon Shines by Day first published by
Speaking Tiger in hardback 2017

The Fate of Butterflies first published by
Speaking Tiger in hardback 2019

This edition first published by Speaking Tiger 2022

ISBN: 978-93-5447-308-1

10 9 8 7 6 5 4 3 2 1

Typeset by SÜRYA, New Delhi
Printed at Chaman Enterprises, New Delhi

WHEN THE MOON SHINES BY DAY

For Kiran Nagarkar, a great storyteller,
this story of our times.

India has changed. Rehana finds her father's books on medieval history have been 'disappeared' from bookstores and libraries. Her young domestic help, Abdul, discovers it is safer to be called Morari Lal in the street, but there is no such protection from vigilante fury for his Dalit friend, Suraj. Kamlesh, a diplomat and writer, comes up against official wrath for his anti-war views. A bomb goes off at Cyrus Batliwala's gallery on the opening day of an art show.

Presiding over this new world is the Director of Cultural Transformation, whose smiling affability masks a relentless agenda to create a Hindu master race.

In this atmosphere, Rehana and her three book-club friends, Nandini, Aruna and Lily, meet every week to discuss a book one of them has chosen—their oasis of peace amidst the harshness of reality—even as Rehana's German friend, Franz Rohner, haunted by his country's Nazi past, warns her of what is to come. All revolutions, he wryly observes, follow the same path. But is India about to prove him wrong?

In this brilliant, dystopian satire, Nayantara Sahgal draws a telling portrait of our times.

The woman was at an angle that made a slanting question mark of her figure—a tilt at which it was impossible to stand, much less take a step forward, which was what the tip of one foot was doing. Her garment fell curving from shoulder to hip, flared out behind her knee and swirled round to her ankle. The thick-looking stuff of it could not possibly have that fluid flow and flare, yet it did. Her figure was in profile, but her face turned outward showing slits for eyes and mouth under a head of elaborately arranged hair pierced by the long straight ornamental sticks that adorn Japanese headdresses.

The scroll hung on her bedroom wall where she could see it first thing in the morning when she opened her eyes. Its contradictions made mysterious artistic sense. The weighty cloth dipped and flowed airily. The figure's moving foot stood still. All of which connected it with the Japanese author's book she had chosen for discussion at the book get-together today.

'He's a British national, Rehana, so you can't call him a Japanese author, and we had a British book last time,' Nandini had objected.

True enough, but the novel had been a favourite of Rehana's since she had read it years ago when it first came out. No setting could be more English—the Lord and Lady, inherited acres, the manor with its vast retinue of maids, footmen, butler. Aristocracy and hierarchy in its heyday in an atmosphere of forever more. Britain in the 1930s. Then who would have expected such a noiseless Japanese way of unravelling such an English story? It was the way the two melled—like Yehudi Menuhin's violin and Ravi Shankar's sitar making music together—that made the book a magical read. You could hear a pin drop in the Japanese stillness of the storytelling, however English the story.

The book club had been Nandini's idea. She had her doubts about discussing such an old novel when they could hardly keep up with all the new books coming out. Rehana had persuaded her to count it as new since it was a new revised edition. It had a special fascination for her, having grown up with her father's memories of the 1930s when he was a student in London. Peacetime though it was, the Hitler-Mussolini arsenal of terrifying newly minted armaments was pounding Spain's towns and Spanish lives to rubble in support of the generalissimo who had overthrown Spain's elected government. The two dictators had chosen the Iberian peninsula to try out their weapons for war-worthiness.

'Didn't any country help the Spanish republic?' she had asked her father.

Not a single country did, he had said, still angry years later about Europe's callous indifference. Europe's democracies sat by and watched. It's not our war, they said. For them it was dust, death and foreign furore far south. It was civil war on the outer edge of Europe in a country that was European by a hair's breadth. The mess down there was being taken care of by the Europeans who knew what to do about it. It was nothing to worry about as Generalissimo Franco was getting all the support he needed. So it was not surprising, Rehana recalled when she re-read the novel she had chosen, that war did not figure in conversation at the manor. For the manor life carried on as it always had and always would. English teas on green English lawns, breakfasts on a sideboard loaded with bacon, kidneys, kippers, kedgeree and left half uneaten, and five-course black-tie dinners to which the men who governed England came. The centipedal crawl of fascism slithering through the story was conspicuous by its absence from the manor's pleasant days and nights.

Papa had clarified that though no government had moved a muscle to help the beleaguered Spanish republic, thousands of volunteers from many countries had gone to fight for Spain. But courage, conviction and passion were up against the deadliest war machine the world had ever seen and they were easy prey for the armed fury let loose on Spain by Franco's friends.

His own personal memory of the time was of his seventeen-year-old self jammed in the crowd of thousands in Trafalgar Square at the meeting organized by the republic's supporters. From where he stood, straining to see above the higher heads in front of him, he saw the slim silhouette of an Indian in a black shervani and black Gandhi cap speaking from a platform below Nelson's statue. The speaker had one arm flung out making its passionate point. He was telling them he had just come back from Barcelona.

'There I entered this Europe of conflict. There I remained for five days and watched the bombs fall nightly from the air. There in the midst of want and destruction I felt more at peace with myself than anywhere else in Europe. There was light there, the light of courage and determination and of doing something worthwhile. Spain was not Spain only but a world locked in a death struggle with the barbarian hordes of reaction and brutal violence. Spain and Czechoslovakia represented to me precious values in life. If I deserted them, what would I cherish in India? For what kind of freedom do we struggle?'

Nehru's words had found a resounding echo in the crowd.

The rehearsal in Spain for the world war to come, said Papa, would have been wiped clear out of human memory if it hadn't been for the novels written about it; if the desperate screams of the dying and the terror engulfing the city of

Guernica had not survived in Picasso's painting of Guernica being pulverized one Monday afternoon in April 1937. What if only the destroyers' versions had survived? In one of these the Nazi commander of the aerial bombardment had noted triumphantly in his diary: 'Guernica, a city with five thousand residents, has been literally razed to the ground. Bomb craters can be seen in the streets. Simply wonderful.' In another, a Nazi general had recorded that combat experience in the field like this trial run was far more useful than ten years of military training in peacetime. And Generalissimo Franco's version let it be known it was retreating republicans who had destroyed the city.

That is why novels have to be written, Rehana, and paintings have to be painted, Papa had said. Without art and literature we would never know the truth.

He was a historian himself but he had a personal interest in works of art because his closest friend, Nikhil, was a well-known artist, and as time went on, one of the best.

~

Kamlesh was looking forward to lunch. It was three years since he and Franz Rohner had met. They had had Fellowships at the Lyleford Institute in New York and had foregathered with other Fellows in the central hall for convivial get-togethers over vintage sherries at midday—a welcome break from a morning's concentration. Sometimes he and Franz had carried on talking over lunch in the institute's dining room. Franz was lively company and his subject was revolutions—French, Russian, Italian, German, and other historic convulsions of the Left or Right. What had made his books popular reading was his entertaining approach. He could describe a horrifying event in excruciating detail in language that made an absurdity of it. Kamlesh had seen that done brilliantly on film. Chaplin's Hitler had been reduced to idiotic antics in *The Great Dictator*, but no one had done quite this in writing. He couldn't remember which revolution Franz had been working on at the institute, but that project had now been published and he was in India for the launch of its Indian edition.

Kamlesh went through security at the entrance and walked into the lobby of the Ashwin, the newly opened hotel where Franz's publisher had put him up. The publisher was doing him proud. Five-star was the norm; the Ashwin was a six-star. Obviously he was certain of record sales. It was his own first time in the hotel and he glanced around the immense high-ceilinged crystal-chandeliered lobby. Who invented chandeliers? It must take a high-wire trapeze act to clean them. The purpose of chandeliers in their heavenly abode might well be to show they are on high and you are below and make sure you know the difference. Soaring walls and glass-like expanses of floor gleamed golden-beige under concealed lighting. Other people had built Taj Mahals and the like. This must be a monument to the prosperity we didn't yet have. The fountain in the middle of the lobby had a low marble surround you could sit on and peer down into its marble base studded with clusters of what looked like rubies, emeralds and sapphires glinting and glimmering in a chandelier's underwater light. Several hotel guests standing beside him were admiring the jewelled effect. A child leaned over too far and was yanked back by a parental hand to keep her from toppling over. Her shriek startled Kamlesh out of his reverie. Hotel staff were moving around, guests were checking out, checking in. Suitcases were being wheeled in, baggage was being trundled out on trolleys. The lobby was as busy and bustling with activity as any hotel lobby. Bemused by its appearance of immense emptiness, he hadn't noticed. Strange what the arrangement of bricks and stone known as architecture could do.

The reception counter was brightly lit. The man behind it said 'Bharat Mata ki Jai' and Kamlesh asked for Franz's room number. He was told the gentleman was awaiting him in the dining room. Directed to the distant end of the lobby he stopped on the way to look into the bookshop and saw copies of Franz's book prominently displayed beside shiny hardcovers of *Mein Kampf*. The irony of the Nazi bible being displayed alongside Franz's book—Franz who was famous for satirizing the Fuhrer and his kind—made Kamlesh smile. The dining room was well filled but Kamlesh spotted Franz at once. There he was, at a window table, handsomely blond, sitting straight and tall in spite of his age. There had never been any scholarly slouch about him. He had not mentioned his wife would be with him but she was there beside him and Kamlesh was struck once again by their resemblance to each other. One could easily take them for brother and sister. They had the same grey-blond good looks, blue eyes and, at least in his own inexpert judgement, a Scandinavian more than a German fairness.

Greetings and handshakes were boisterous and Kamlesh sat down opposite Gerda. Catching up waited till they had ordered, and there was no ordering until the menu had been seriously perused, as had the menu in the Lyleford dining room. The maitre d' waved the waiter away, set menus before them himself and stood by for their order. Franz ruled out salad, causing Gerda to courteously explain, 'You see, we have been advised not to eat raw vegetables in India, and fruit only if we have peeled it ourselves.' The maitre d' assured them the fruit and vegetables were grown on Mr Ashwin's own farm and, raw or cooked, they were most safe. An array of crisp greens arrived while Franz and Gerda, their heads lowered and touching over the menu, conferred lengthily about the main course and decided on seafood. Someone had told Franz there was a fish restaurant not far from here that had lobsters flown fresh and live, not frozen, from the west coast. It made all the difference to the flavour. They brought these live creatures to your table in a clay pot of water for you to choose one before they took it away and plunged it into boiling water. Of course they couldn't bring clay pots around in this dining room but the maitre d' assured them that here, too, they got consignments of freshly caught lobster flown up from the coast and cooked alive on demand. Kamlesh remembered that Franz was as particular about what he ate as about his views on revolutions, and had the same flair for dissecting every aspect of both. His own order of filet of sole, easy to slice and eat, compared tamely with the ritual of hot melted butter drizzled onto lobster, succulent white flesh gouged out of its shell by the forkful and lifted again and again to waiting expectant mouths, while eyelids drooped in blissful acknowledgment of expectation fulfilled.

'So how are things going on here?' asked Franz between mouthfuls.

A vague general answer would not do. Kamlesh knew Franz's practical mind dealt in verifiable specifics. Seeing the maitre d' engaged elsewhere in the dining room, he tried to be specific about something as intangible as atmosphere, which was all he had to go by. Did atmosphere have a beginning? Was it the bullets that bloodied a prayer ground in January 1948? Or the prancing and capering years later on the wrecked and shattered dome of a mosque? Or after that when death danced through a city? Or long before any of that? When had it begun?

Kamlesh heard himself pondering possibilities but he must have sounded factual enough because in an abrupt change of mood Franz said sharply, 'Religion joined to nation is a marriage made in hell. We know this in Germany.'

Religion and Germany? What had religion to do with Germany? What was Franz talking about? But the maitre d' arrived to enquire if all was satisfactory. It was. Their plates were removed and an unpronounceable dessert was pointed out on the menu. All three of them agreed to it, and then Franz wanted to know what he was writing.

At the Lyleford Institute Kamlesh had been completing the book he had titled *Genie Out of the Bottle*. Hardly a suitable title for the Non-Aligned Movement, his publisher, Sudhir, had objected. But it was just right for the magician's act it had been, Kamlesh had argued, and quoted a poet who had got to the heart and soul of it. Richard Wright, black American, had written of the men who launched the Movement at Bandung: 'Only black, brown and yellow men could have felt the need for such a meeting. There was something extra-political, extra-social, almost extra-human about it. It smacked of tidal waves, of natural forces. The agenda and the subject matter had been written for centuries in the blood and bones of the participants.' Poets will be poets, Sudhir had shrugged, unimpressed, but what had poetry to do with politics? Kamlesh knew of moods and moments in history when it inexplicably had, and he had stuck to his title.

'Now that I'm posted back here,' he said, 'I'm working on the Taj Mahal story.'

'What is there to write about the Taj Mahal?' enquired Gerda. 'It is there to see and wonder at.'

Not only, Kamlesh told her. It had been remarked on by foreign travellers from far and wide. No Mughal building, maybe no building anywhere, had attracted so much interest. He was no architect himself. but was there anyone who remained unaffected by extraordinary architecture? Walk into the Duomo in Milan and be spellbound. Stand on a sidewalk in New York, look up at a skyscraper and feel your head spin. Let your eyes encircle the serene symmetry of a mosque.

'But what about the romance? I hope you will

not leave out the romance, the love story which is the reason for it.'

He assured her he would not, and asked Franz which revolution his new book was about.

'It is about several. It is a jumble. What does it matter which one? After all they are much the same.'

This was a subject they had argued about before, a losing battle for Kamlesh whose contention that they were poles apart in ideas and aims cut no ice with Franz.

'Once in power they are the same,' said Franz. 'Blood brothers could not be more alike. And whose atrocities are worse we do not know. This kaiserschmarn is excellent.'

'Delicious,' breathed Gerda, spooning more whipped cream on the scramble of pancake and apple sauce on her plate, 'and fancy finding a Bavarian dessert here.'

Going back to atrocities, Kamlesh observed that some had been worse than others.

'As we know,' Franz agreed, but added, 'The human race has been created cruel. How else to explain the family outings to watch hangings and beheadings, or the lusty cheers when the guillotine struck. But wait, let me think of a homemade example, an ordinary family custom…like your plain and simple widow-burning used to be.' And he came up with foot-binding. 'Note the scientific care with which it was done. First cutting the woman's toenails and soaking her feet in hot water to soften up the skin. Then massaging them with alum. After that breaking every toe except the big toe and folding them under the sole of the foot…'

'Please, Franz,' Gerda pleaded with an anguished intensity that went deeper than a protest against these gory details. It came to Kamlesh that Franz's recital chillingly lacked the saving grace of his trademark humour.

'Then the feet are tightly bound to break the arches. After this they are laid into shoes designed for feet that will never walk again. For a thousand years they will only hobble. And if you ask, is this not cruelty? they will be surprised. No, no, it is a household practice to keep her in her womanly place. Torture comes naturally to the human species and it begins at home. How scientifically it is planned, Kamlesh, to achieve the desired result—the tool to break the toes, the shoe for what the foot has become. My dear Kamlesh, in matters of cruelty I am beyond surprise.'

They finished their coffee in silence. The silence lengthened. A waiter brought marzipan candies. Kamlesh tried to think of something to say.

'What will you write next?' he finally asked.

Gerda's hands were lying limply on the table. Franz covered them with one of his own, as if in apology. He sounded more like himself when he spoke.

'I am thinking of writing about a family matter. Did we tell you we will not be returning directly to Europe after our time here? We are planning to take a cruise from Mumbai to wherever it takes us. Gerda will swim and lie in the sun. I will recollect and scribble. In the evenings we will drink and dance the nights away.'

Kamlesh took leave of them in the lobby, saying he would be there at the book launch the following evening.

~

Rehana never knew how to describe Nikhil's paintings. They had a physical strength one was not prepared for from paint laid on canvas. Dense, intense colour and all the shades of its absence gave his paintings a violence that spoke. You saw the filth-crusted plodding feet, the sweat and grime with new astonished eyes. So, too, the one-legged beggar girl hopping in the treacherous inches between two rows of cars. So, too, the grim grey interior of some confine where a naked woman lies. Her arms have been dragged up, manacled at the wrists and roped to something further up. Her mouth gapes in a scream you can hear being torn out of it by a paintbrush that makes remorseless use of dark and light.

A critic once asked Nikhil why he was so obsessed with dismal subjects and he had retorted that his obsession was with colour. Subjects were what happened to be there. Except of course the giant loaf of bread that filled the cloudless sky of one canvas. The loaf is mightily risen and the heavenly halo encircling it is blindingly luminous. On earth far below it a tiny man in a langot lies prostrate, face-down in slush. His ribs poke through his skin like you see in emaciated cattle. His mud-spattered arms grope forward straining to join his palms in prayer.

'What is this celestial loaf supposed to mean?' Papa had demanded.

'It means what you see: "For the poor man God is a loaf of bread". Except that Gandhi got it wrong. This poor wretch shouldn't be worshipping a "double roti" he's never heard of. He should be praying to a chappati.' Nikhil laughed his infectious irresistible laugh.

The sound of his laughter filled food-and-drink evenings at home. He and her parents spoke the tri-language that was natural to them, starting in one language, slipping into another if it was better suited to what they were describing. Rehana had grown up believing their interwoven Hindi-Urdu-English was one and the same entrancing language. They had named her Rehana because they liked the sound of it. Like their language, their world had no frontiers either. What they knew of Europe they had made their own. Nikhil said Prague was Europe's most beautiful city, Mama said Budapest. Whichever was, they agreed Europe's most beautiful people were born of Europe's collision with Asia. The magic was in the mix.

The heartbreaking news coming over the radio from a Europe being devastated by war had moved them to tears and had taught Rehana that when such things happen the heart has no boundaries. She heard them recall the speaker at Trafalgar Square who had made the Nazi war on Spain and the invasion of Czechoslovakia his own grim personal concern. 'Spain and Czechoslovakia represented to me precious values in life,' he had said, 'If I deserted them, what would I cherish in India? For what kind of freedom do we struggle?' For them his impassioned avowal became a call to arms of another kind, drawing them into Gandhi's weaponless fight for freedom from British rule.

Nikhil had served one long sentence, her parents two each for the treason of refusing allegiance to the King Emperor. What had it felt like hearing the massive iron jail gate clang shut behind you, having your watch, pen, wallet confiscated, even your handkerchief lest it be hiding subversion, and being marched to a barrack where another iron gate clanged shut, locking you and years of your life behind stone walls? Rehana marvelled at the ruggedness of their idealism and the times that had made it possible. The distance between then and now wasn't all that long but suddenly the present had no past. Papa's books on medieval India were gone from shop shelves, struck off curriculums and dropped from his publisher's list. Kamlesh had helped her to trace and collect as many as they could locate and she had stored them in two old leather suitcases that would take their weight.

Occupied with their work and the fullness of their lives after freedom, her parents had not harked back to their jailed years. When freedom came, song, dance, paint, poetry and much else cast off the shackles of what had gone before. An example had been set by the war that had broken free of war's violent history when Gandhi replaced it with civil disobedience and made non-violence the command that sent men and women into battle unarmed, something new under the sun.

The atmosphere of newness was electric. No one was harking back. Rehana would never have known what her parents had gone through during the years of struggle if it hadn't been for the diary Mama had kept of her last imprisonment. The only mention she had ever made of it was that she had been one of a hundred thousand prisoners and what had kept her going was the knowledge of that unknown unseen comradeship. Rehana still re-read bits of the diary from time to time though it was no less hurtful each time:

> *13 August 1942*: I was conducted to the old familiar barrack. I had been away from this barrack for a year and a half and returning to it seemed a continuation of my second term in prison. It was 3:15 am. I spread my bedding on the ground, was locked in, and my second term of prison life began. My head ached badly and the throbbing in my temples prevented sleep. There is no water, no sanitary arrangements, nothing at all. In the morning

I got a little water from the convicts' bathing tap and washed my face. Towards noon some raw rations arrived but no coal, so cooking was not possible. Later with a convict's help I tried to make a small fire of twigs but the fire would not light. It is now six, lock-up time. The matron enquires what I will be having for dinner. I said what could I eat when there was nothing to eat. So ends the first day of my second term of imprisonment.

14 August 1942: Some raw rations have arrived on my second day, some vegetables and a bundle of firewood. The rations are mildewed and are mixed with grit and dirt, tiny stones and even a spider, maybe to make up the weight of what we are allowed. I cook it and I am so hungry that I eat it. So far there are no rats but they will come. Last time a family of rats had the run of the place.

Every now and again shouts of 'Inquilab Zindabad' and other slogans come to me from the men's barrack over the wall. I feel less lonely after that and, in a way, happier. Comfort, happiness, freedom, how meaningless these words have become.

16 August 1942: A woman who is in for murder told me she killed her husband because he thrashed her and starved her. The six-week-old baby girl she brought to jail with her died, and she had to leave her two-year-old son behind. She has not seen him since then. He is now eleven and she cries for him.

18 August 1942: There is a new rule for political prisoners. We will not be permitted newspapers, letters, interviews or any article from home. Jail clothes will be provided. Our allowance will be reduced from twelve annas to nine annas per day.

19 August 1942: This barrack is rectangular and made to accommodate twelve or more convicts. There are gratings along each side. The ceiling falls in chunks and makes a mess on the cot and on the floor. The door is bolted and locked every night. One side of the barrack is raised four steps from the ground and serves as a latrine after lock-up. I keep my jail cot at the furthest end of the barrack from the latrine. We are surrounded by high walls which shut out even the trees.

There is a door between my yard and the adjoining yard. The cells there are unfit for any human being. There is a woman there now who I can hear wailing through the day and the night. It is a horrible sound, the wail of a prisoner who has lost all hope and is afraid. Hearing it I haven't been able to sleep. When I finally did I dreamt I was in a solitary cell. It was hardly high enough for me to stand up in and by stretching my arms sideways I could touch the walls on either side. I cried to get out but the cell was locked and there was no escape. After this dream I couldn't sleep. A rhyme read long ago came to my mind:

> As he went through cold Bath fields
> he saw a solitary cell
> And the Devil was pleased, for it gave
> him a hint
> For improving the prisons in Hell.

> *22 August 1942*: The days are incredibly long and prison nights surely contain more hours than any others. In the evenings I like to sit near my grating and watch the drifting clouds pass in the sky and wait for the stars to come out. So far there is no moon but I wait for her to send a silver beam into my barrack by way of greeting and to show that she remembers me.

Abdul, her servant, interrupted her reading. She could never remember to call him Morari Lal, the name he had given to shopkeepers and street vendors in the bazaar. With the alertness essential for survival, he had heard before she did that Mussalmans were now regarded as outsiders who must wear a badge and live in a far-off settlement too far from his work here. So it was better to be Morari Lal in the street. Abdul was eighteen and had come a year ago from Jharkhand. It was not hard to imagine how he must have travelled. Rehana could see him in the train, crushed between bodies on a bench packed with bodies. He is welded to the bench. In his waking sleep his head jerks up and down and lurches sideways, hitting his neighbour's as the train rocks and jolts on its westward track. This punishment is called travel and there is no knowing what lies at the end of it. Station stops ease the numbness in his arms and legs and give him six minutes to swallow hot sweet tea and buy the food his coins allow. He chews it in cautious mouthfuls, making it last. There has never been enough of it to eat ravenously or he would have grown to his full height. If migrants migrate it must be because they must. Here the migrant network directs him to jobs and so to her house. He helps Gangu in the kitchen and does all the housework. He hasn't taken a holiday to go home. When she asked him why, he said in his rapid-fire way: mother-father dead in firing when village land seized by mining company, grandmother useless with weeping, sisters already given in marriage, uncle put him on train, giving her to understand there is no home to go back to.

Rehana had shown him how to work the washing machine. Minutes later he was still squatted in front of it watching blouses and brassieres, petticoats, towels, sheets and pillowcases being hurled around, which she had never thought of as an enthralling sight.

'Bibi,' Abdul told her, not for the first time, 'basement is damp. Abba-jan sahib's books should not be there.'

But where else could she store them, save them? Abdul emptied the suitcases every few days and spread the books out in the sun to save them from mildew and she dreamed of a dignified setting for Papa's life's work, a library where his books would be catalogued, numbered, taken out and kept in circulation.

The book discussion this afternoon at Nandini's was argumentative, as it often was. The four of them were in their late forties, all but herself with grown sons and daughters now on their own, studying or starting work. Nandini was the only one who was maternally inclined by nature but even she had not been interested in ruling the world via rocking the cradle as the saying went and had made a fabled success of running the confectionary side of her husband's catering business. Rehana's three close friends made the most of their well-earned release from parenting and all four enjoyed this time-out from the demands of their working lives. But books were more than a casual reason for getting together. They shared a curiosity about the art of story-making, the many and mysterious effects of words on a page that made for the spell-casting joy of literature. It was a time-out Rehana particularly valued because she thought of the three of them as belonging to normal life, and herself not quite, but basking in it through them. Unlike though they were, what they also had in common, or so it seemed to her, was the composure that comes of not having been trained to self-efface, and the book choices they made were interestingly different.

Rehana pointed out her chosen novel's sinister undercurrent which strangely had gone unnoticed in the manor. For the others this aspect of the story, so central to it, didn't ring true. How could the manor not have seen war was coming, especially when the men who governed the country came to dinner? Could they have sat at the dinner table downing vintage port and gone on about grouse-shoots, and their wives in another room about their daughters' debuts in society? Would the manor and its guests not have noticed they were about to be overrun by the tanks rolling over Europe? So, psychologically, it didn't add up. Tea ended with Aruna concluding that not realizing what was so plainly going on all around you couldn't happen in real life, but then of course this was fiction.

Rehana got home and remembered she had promised Kamlesh she would go with him to a book launch he had been invited to and he was coming to pick her up. He and Vineet had been friends and colleagues in the foreign service and he kept in affectionate touch.

~

Kamlesh, by virtue of being the Rohners' friend, and Rehana with him, were given front row seats next to Gerda and Mrs Ashwin, and were warmly greeted. Nalin Ashwin got up from his seat to welcome them. He was not at all what his multi-millions and the size and grandeur of his hotel, or his closeness to the highest in the land, had led Kamlesh to expect. Of medium height, his informal manner was charming and disarming. He told them he had taken a degree in political science at Princeton before going on to management and all that, hence his interest in the author whose work he greatly admired. The auditorium, not the hotel's largest but the one for cultural events, was soon full. Kamlesh guessed these were people who may not have read Franz, but had certainly heard about him, and had come to be entertained. Franz didn't disappoint them. He read a witty extract from his new book that set a light-hearted mood for the evening.

'Welcome to India, Mr Rohner,' smiled Nalin Ashwin in the conversation that followed, 'you are here at the best possible time. I won't call it a revolution, knowing your own suspicion of the word'—a nod of cheerful acknowledgement from Franz Rohner—'but a great cultural transformation. May I say we have learned a lot from the revival and rebirth of Germany between the wars—especially your pride in your Germanness. If sitting here on this stage you could look back and refashion the phenomenal rise of Germany, would you have kept its power at home and not advanced it across Europe—after reclaiming Austria and Czechoslovakia, of course, because those countries were part-German anyway.'

Franz heartily agreed that occupying Austria, Belgium, Holland, Czechoslovakia, Luxemburg, Poland, Norway, Denmark, Greece and Yugoslavia had not been a good idea. And the Czechs and Austrians too, had most certainly not enjoyed being occupied, part-German or part anything else that they might have been. We are all part something else, are we not? Who is purely one thing? And as for going too far, that is the trouble with revolutions.

Franz's turn of phrase and the string of occupied countries he ticked off on the raised fingers of both hands brought a collective chuckle from the audience.

'The other trouble with revolutions is, they are so boring. There was a novel in Stalin's time called *Cement.* You have guessed it, it was about cement. And then all the repetition. We had our Heil Hitlering. Spain went one better with ' Viva Generalissimo Franco Franco Franco'—yes, three Francos at a time. They all had the same stiff-armed salute'—Franz stood up and shot out his arm to demonstrate it—'but the Italians went one better. The hailing and heiling was not enough for them. As we know, they have music in their souls so they also hailed their Duce and 'fascismo' with song.'

To the audience's delight he sang it:

'Giovinezza, giovinezza
Primavera di belleza
Nel fascismo e la salvezza
Della nostra liberta
Per Benito Mussolini
Eia eia alala!'

The applause was enthusiastic and prolonged. Nalin joined in it. When it subsided he said, 'But, Mr Rohner, the truth is that many at that time looked to Italy and Germany for inspiration. It was Mussolini who advised our leader B.S. Moonje to give our youth sound military training when Moonje had an audience with him in the Palazzo Venzia in 1934. From the age of six a child's mind must be made ready for war, he said. Peace had to be based on millions of steel bayonets. Those were his very words. Moonje took them to heart and when he came home he set up the recruiting and training of children and youths for an armed militia like Mussolini's Balillas. To give them their due, can we deny that the two dictators, yours and the Italian, were greatly admired at one time?'

'Indeed they were,' agreed Franz, 'So was the crinoline. This was a hoop of a garment made of wire that swung out like a circular cage around the woman. Over it went a skirt and under it were petticoats upon petticoats made of horse's hair to hold the cage in place. When she sat down the hoop flew up so she must lower herself with caution. After the crinoline came the bustle. This was a lump of padding on her behind under her skirt to make her derriere stick out like a table in a posture that pushed her breast out in front. Breast out front, rump out behind. And both these were high fashion. They, too, were greatly admired—at one time.'

There was a lone cackle, then an extended roar of laughter from his listeners before the conversation could resume.

'Your books have parodied revolutions and you make them sound alike. But are they?' asked Nalin.

'Are they not?' Franz spread his hands wide. 'It has all happened before and it keeps happening, always as before. It is tiresome how they copycat each other, even to their craze for uniforms to carry out their commands. Black Shirts, Brown

Shirts. This is why a wise observer of that time wrote: "Three cheers for dear old Gandhi, Who wears no shirt at all!"'

The unfamiliar limerick caused more mirth.

Nalin persisted goodnaturedly, enjoying his task, 'We know from your books it's the violence you object to, but all through history it has been understood that the end justifies the means. As everyone knows, you can't make an omelette without breaking eggs.'

'Indeed you cannot, so why make an omelette? Is it not time to boil the eggs instead?'

More hilarity in which Nalin joined. When it died down he went on, 'Since you say they are all the same, how would you describe revolutions in a nutshell?'

Franz pondered this. 'In a nutshell, let me see. One and all, they come from the top,' he began. 'So in a nutshell, are they not the man who mounts his woman with no please-may-I, gallops to glory, rolls off his mount and snores himself to sleep? And the woman? Ah, the woman! She lies awake plotting how to kill him.'

After a second's shock, shouts of laughter erupted. When Nalin could make himself heard he said he assumed the woman is 'the people'. But didn't the people benefit at all from revolution? Oh yes, some few did, Franz conceded, oh yes, beyond their wildest dreams.

The quantity of books laid out were signed and sold and orders placed for more. At cocktails afterwards, Gerda told Arati Ashwin what a surprise it had been finding a Bavarian dessert on the menu and Arati said she collected national desserts when she travelled abroad with her husband. It was a hobby of hers and her dessert cookbook had done very well. Before leaving she told Gerda there would be a car at the Rohners' disposal for their shopping and sightseeing all the days they were here.

Rehana picked a morsel of camembert toothpicked to a wafer off the tray being offered, and another before the tray moved on. The man beside her took a couple too.

'These are very good,' he said, and like people at cocktail parties who don't know each other and will never meet again, they chatted pleasantly about nothing in particular.

Rehana was glad she had agreed to come with Kamlesh. She had been feeling bleak and miserable since Papa's books had been disappeared. Being among people in anonymous undemanding company helped. The author's well-known humour had had the curious effect of drawing her attention to what lay unspoken beneath it. Something about his talk had revived a forgotten faith. Suddenly, there he was, standing tall and striking in front of her, telling her Kamlesh had informed him she was the daughter of the famous historian whose work he knew well. Rehana caught her breath. She had a longing to reach up and fling her arms around him in sheer joy. She accepted the glass he took off a tray and handed her, saying, 'So should we not drink to your father?' This time she could have wept, but again for sheer joy. She had no idea what she was drinking, only that it was going to her head. She was talking animatedly to the German with the complete confidence of being understood and he was listening intently to what she was saying.

He invited her to stay on and dine with him and Gerda as Kamlesh was doing. They ate duck l'orange and other delectable dishes selected by him from the French menu. Superbly dined and wined, their talk drifted, unserious, unhurried. Franz turned vaguely philosophical.

'Purity,' he said, 'does not exist. It is a chimera, a dangerous, absurd imagining. No one and nothing is just one thing. Blood, culture, our past, our present, they are all mixed. Did Italy bring noodles to China or the other way round? Is a summer's day the temperature on the thermometer or is it a breeze, a bird, a butterfly…'

'He gets like that,' said Gerda lovingly,

slipping her arm through his and rubbing her cheek against his shirt sleeve, 'especially after such a meal.'

The band was playing nostalgic old favourites. Couples on the dance floor were in slow slumberous motion, dancing cheek to cheek. The crooner at the mike twitched her hips to the beat and huskily confessed:

When love walks in
And takes you for a spin
Ooo la la la, c'est magnifique!
And when once more he whispers 'Je t'adore'
C'est magnifique!

They agreed it was the perfect ending to Franz's book launch.

~

Aruna had brought a copy of Arati Ashwin's cookbook to show them at their book get-together. It was a present from a friend and clearly a collector's item. They passed it around. Rehana's hand glided over the pearly texture of its pages and its mouthwatering illustrations of unheard-of desserts.

'She won't be travelling for a while,' Aruna informed them. 'She's expecting. It was in the papers. It said she already has three but that Baba Ghanshyam who's advising on culture has called on patriotic Hindus to have at least five and she wants to set an example.'

'What do you think of your lot being told to stay pregnant? Looks like your Ghanshyam Baba and my Pope see eye to eye on womb control,' Lily said.

'Actually it's nothing new,' Rehana reflected, 'Wombs have been controlled by popes and imams and husbands since time began. By governments too. What about China's one-child policy that made women report their periods every month?'

'It's crazy,' said Lily, but it reminded her to tell them her news. Arati Ashwin had heard she designed elegant wear for an exclusive boutique that had its own outlet in Harrods. She had come to the boutique that morning and asked Lily to design a glamorous maternity wardrobe for her. She said pregnant women didn't have to look dowdy and saris were all wrong with all that cloth bunched up around one's middle. Looking glamorous would encourage women to have more babies.

Nandini called them to attention. She poured Flowery Orange Pekoe and they got on to the novel Lily had chosen. It was a new one by a feminist author about a woman in search of orgasm. Jennie hadn't realized what she was missing until she and her husband went to Rome on a holiday and saw Bernini's statue of Santa Teresa d'Avila. Rick who wasn't much of a sightseer and was good and ready for beer and lunch, took a brief look and strolled on.

Jennie hung back as she always did, wanting to get her sightseeing's money's worth. She fetched the tourist booklet out of her shoulder bag and found the page about the sixteenth-century nun. It informed her this was a must-see sculpture. It was Bernini's masterwork. Here it is then. The marble nun appears to be leaning way back in a swoon with one foot dangling off the platform she's sitting on. Her eyes are half closed and her mouth is half open. The guide book spelled out the swoon in Santa Teresa's own words: 'The pain was so strong that it made me utter several moans; and so excessive was the sweetness caused me by this intense pain that one can never wish it to cease…' Evidently Jesus Christ had promised her, 'If I had not created heaven, I would create it for you alone,' and here it is, heaven on earth for her alone.

A nun of all people, for Pete's sake, had this delirious dementing surrender to passion, never mind that it was only for Jesus Christ: 'Her body and spirit are in the throes of rapture,' read Jennie, 'happiness and pain alternating in a fearful fiery all-consuming glow. Such is her ecstasy in climax that her body is literally lifted up before it falls unconscious.' If this was orgasm, Jennie hadn't had one, nothing like. She was very thoughtful as she caught up with Rick and all through their spaghetti carbonara.

The rest of the novel tells of Jennie's adventures in pursuit of ecstasy. There are lovers and there are orgasms. Delicious outer ones, inner ones that take her by storm, on and off furniture and flat on the floor. And then there's that unexpected one arriving after what she had thought was the final one. Jennie is never exactly in the 'throes' of the nun's rapture but near enough. Jennie is Jennie-in-Wonderland.

'What really got me about the story,' said Lily, 'is how cheery it is all the way through. Nothing happens to interfere with the glorious time she's having. I found that exhilarating, and quite uplifting.'

Nandini, incredulous, asked, 'What's uplifting about it?'

'The contrast, of course. Women trudge behind men, they eat after men, they get less to eat than men, they do pujas for men, they stay hungry keeping fasts for men, they get killed before they're born, they are divorced at the drop of a hat, they can't leave home except in thick black shrouds, and they'd better be Virgin Marys or else.' Lily paused, then she said, 'And if that isn't enough, they get butchered to prevent them from having orgasms. No clitoris, no orgasm. What a life. So three cheers for Jennie.'

Silencing though that last horrifying fact was, Nandini, who had to get back to her office to oversee a wedding order, brought attention back to the book. She didn't know why feminist writers had to exaggerate so much to make their point. There was no need to give Jennie that many lovers. One or two would have sounded more convincing. And all those acrobatic goings-on with arms and legs thrown about and wound around in who-cares abandon were a bit much. Not a word about Rick while Jennie was whooping it up. What must the poor man have been going through?

'What do you think, Rehana?'

Rehana had been thinking of the unfairness of it, the nun having it all without stirring, so it was the power of imagination yet again, wasn't it? But that aside, all those acrobatics made Lady Chatterley sound positively stodgy and staid. Sex had come a long way since Lady Chatterley. It showed how much literary times had changed, and that sometimes things did change for the better.

For Aruna the most unconvincing part of the novel was Jennie and Rick staying married as if nothing had happened. 'It's preposterous. It would be impossible in real life.'

'I don't know about that,' countered Lily blandly. 'After all, Jennie and Rick are terribly fond of each other. Why should they break up? And adultery never breaks up a marriage, only knowing about it does.'

After this conclusion, Lily added, displaying her satisfaction with a book she had thoroughly enjoyed reading, 'Come to think of it, it's the story of holy matrimony, only the other way round.'

~

Rehana got home to find Abdul watering the well-weeded little lawn and the flower beds in bloom on two sides of it where he had planted a mismatching riot of flowers, tall and tiny, sturdy and fragile, delicate pastels alongside glaring reds and purples. It looked like a state of barely controlled chaos. Tiger lilies towering over phlox would leave any gardener in shock. Abdul was very pleased with it, marvelling at what had come through the earth at his bidding.

Her parents had built this house in the days when prices in this coveted area were affordable and she had grown up in it. With Vineet in the foreign service, they were out of India for most of their married life until illness cut short his career. They were both walkers and one of the pleasures of being posted abroad had been discovering an unknown city on foot. In Vineet's spare time they had taken walks through unfamiliar street sights and sounds, stopped for coffee or a bite to eat at a sidewalk café and sat there a while, complete in each other's company. The moments she could bear to remember were moments such as these.

The illness that took him was stealthy and ruthless. A creeping paralysis disabled him by degrees until the only movement left to him was to nod his head. At the very last, his face immobilized, he could only blink. She had given thanks for his death when it came and she could let herself break down into helpless unstoppable mourning. Grief is long-lasting, rebellious, everlasting. But like everything that becomes familiar, one starts noticing it less.

Every mourner before her must have wondered if there was life after death, or as some believed, life after life—farfetched, pointless speculations that were no earthly use to those who were left behind. Last week she had been at Lily's for Easter brunch on the day they celebrated the resurrection of Christ. It reminded her of an Easter in Ireland when she and Vineet had gone to church with friends and heard Handel's *Messiah* performed. Gooseflesh had prickled her arms and the church itself had seemed to burst its confines, hard-pressed to contain the majesty of the Hallelujah chorus. Who knew for sure if the crucified prisoner called Jesus of Nazareth had really risen from the tomb? Had he really appeared in the flesh to his disciples on the road to Emmaeus? Had anyone else seen him? But a church had risen for all to see and this victorious rapture had risen for all to hear in praise of him.

This may be all we could ever know about life after death.

Hers was the last house in this tree-shaded lane off the main road. It used to be quiet. Now, with more cars than the road could hold, the incessant rumble and roar of machinery in motion reached her. Stalled in their tracks, a manic bray of horns demanded motion where none was possible. And there were nearer night noises. A rowdy argument, a street quarrel, a drunken brawl. Were voices pitched louder in the night or did they sound louder because it was night? One night a ruckus outside the neighbouring house compelled her out of bed and to her bedroom window. The couple next door were home late from a party. The woman being flung against the iron gate was teetering on her stiletto heels. The street light shone on her sequinned sari. Her husband was slapping her expertly with the back of his hand swinging back and forth across her face until she lost her balance. The next morning she had smiled prettily and waved her jewelled fingers at Rehana through the window of her silver-grey chauffeur-driven palace on wheels. Rehana had waved back.

Around mid-morning next day Cyrus's car drove in. She ran downstairs to be enveloped in his bear hug, and they sat by the garden wall under the shade of the cassia's blossoming branches. It was unusual for Cyrus to arrive unannounced in the middle of a working day. Abdul came out, was given a friendly punch in the midriff and told to provide coffee.

Cyrus owned the art gallery he had inherited from his father and it was Batlivala senior who, in the explosion of energies after independence, had given his controversial opinion: 'Art is what kicks where it hurts' and had championed breakaway art. He had bought and exhibited Nikhil's early work and they had become fast friends. Cyrus, not just his father's son, had become a discerning discoverer in his own right and was entitled to some smugness on that account, but he refused to take himself seriously or to be serious about anything. In Cyrus-fashion he called his art-spotting his poor substitute for not being able to paint. As a schoolboy, he had been driven by a desperation to draw. His drawing master and Papa Batlivala had done their darndest to make an artist of him, but, alas, Cyrus baba had been a hopeless case.

Abdul brought coffee and requested Cyrus to call him Morari Lal. Rehana had to explain why.

'I know the place he would have been sent to,' said Cyrus, 'I've been there. Housing they call it, but it's tenements crammed together, with rooms no bigger than holes in the wall. I went there to find a boy. His name is Hanif. I came across a painting of his quite by chance and I had to find him. He works in a scullery in an eating place nearby. Will he have to spend the rest of his life living in that rathole, washing dirty degchis and plates for a living? That boy is an artist. He must paint. I've got to get him out of there. It's not going to be easy now that he's been listed and already removed to that ghetto.'

The Batlivalas were a wealthy family, and like his father, Cyrus helped and nurtured young and needy artists. To dilute the distressing situation he had described, she said lightly, 'Why haven't you been listed, Cyrus? You're an outsider.'

He wagged an admonishing finger at her. 'You're forgetting history, Rehana. Outsiders were the noisy conquering kind. We smart fellows slipped in quietly much earlier and since we're a dwindling handful we don't count. Actually, who's even heard of us? Let me tell you about my grandpa who was a penniless nobody in London when the First World War started and being the loyal chap he was, he lined up to be recruited to fight for King and empire. When his turn came and he had given his name, the recruiting sergeant at the desk bawled out, "What's your religion?" and grandpa said, "Parsee."

"You mean RC?"

'Grandpa repeated "Parsee".

'The sergeant turned to the uniformed minion standing by his desk, "What in bleeding Hades is that?" to be told, "Ee's one of them blokes wot worships the sun." But to get to the point, dear girl, Nikhil's anniversary is coming up, that is, of his first exhibition with us, and I think we should exhibit what we have of his works again along with the other progressives.'

She gave her enthusiastic approval and said she would be along to help in any way she could.

Cyrus rang a few days later. 'About the boy, I made an appointment with the DCT. There are so many initials floating around, you may not know this stands for Director of Cultural Transformation. He's also in charge of racial purity so the ghetto comes under him. I went to see him yesterday in that new glass-fronted high-rise and I was taken straight through past the front room where hordes were waiting to see him, to his office at the back. It looks out on a spreading lawn with a sprinkler watering the greenest grass and the reddest roses you ever saw. His office was all peace and light. Like a painting by Vermeer, I swear. A bowl of purple pansies on his desk. Pictures of their heroes on the wall behind him. And he couldn't have been more gracious. He gave me cardamom tea and said he's sensitive to aromas, cardamom and other spices, but above all to the seasonal perfumes of his garden. He had inherited his sensitivity. From your father? I asked him. From the ages, he said with a smile. The inheritance of skills is the crowning glory of caste. It fine-tunes each skill to its finest, which is why he can tell one flower's scent from another with his eyes closed, even one rose from another, a yellow from a pink or a white. Well, after that he said he had heard of my good father and knew of my own devotion to art. He wanted to know what he could do for me. When I told him he assured me my concern for this person, whoever he was, was truly praiseworthy and so typical of my community which cared for its own with such well-known compassion and now for this person who was not of my community. But this person whoever he was, was well settled in the housing estate set up for his community, so there was no need to worry on that score. It was a complete arrangement with its own market and shops where they had their own tailors, butchers, barbers and others of their own community to serve their community. People like to be among their own kind, and moving them out of the city had been a safety measure for their own good, with feeling running so high against them. "We cannot forget the pain of invasions, Mr Batlivala, the Turks, Mongols, Mughals, foreigners who interrupted our Hindu history. You may say we are now engaged in wiping out that painful memory and returning our nation by all possible means to its racial and religious purity. Is that not plain justice? That is the cultural transformation we are bringing about.

"Notwithstanding all that, Mr Batlivala, I would have done my best to grant your request, only now the matter of a separate estate for his community has passed into law so with deep regret my hands are tied."

'Then, Rehana, he got up and walked with me to the door and out to the verandah and pointed with pride to the red rose beds and in case I hadn't noticed them, the blush-pink beauties rambling up the garden wall. "Other than this matter if there is anything else I can do..." So we said Bharat Mata ki Jai to each other and I came away.'

'Well then,' she said resignedly, 'there's nothing to be done.'

'I've already done what had to be done. I abducted the boy. I went there, put him and his mother and their belongings into my car and drove off. There was nobody around.'

She might have guessed Cyrus would find his

own way out of an intractable problem but she had not been prepared for law-breaking. Ignoring her alarm he said, 'Hanif is safe with me for the moment but I'll have to find him and his mother a place somewhere soon where he can earn as well as be able to paint. His mother is a tailor and has her sewing machine with her so she will be able to carry on her tailoring.'

'But Cyrus—'

'No buts, Rehana, think ahead,' and he rang off.

~

Nandini was thinking of choosing non-fiction as her book choice for a change, and then for a real change why not ask the author to come and talk to them?

'But four people isn't exactly an audience,' she admitted ruefully, 'so it wouldn't be worthwhile for the writer. No one would come.'

Aruna agreed it was out of the question. 'Authors can be tricky about their importance. At the festival here last year there was one who refused to share the stage with another author. He wanted to perform solo. One would think he'd created the world instead of a book.'

She was a Member of Parliament and brought books that would not have otherwise come to their notice. 'There's an interesting one I wish we could read. The review said it was about the very latest research on populations and that ours like most others has come out of migrations. In other words we're not a pure race polluted by later comers. The writer has been arrested.'

'What for? Under what law can they do that?' they clamoured.

'Under the law against dangerous thoughts. And he's in solitary confinement so that he doesn't infect others. Some of us in Parliament are working for his release.'

'If there's anything I can do. . .' said Rehana

and Aruna nodded, saying she would be in touch.

They would have parted unhappily if Rehana, accustomed to reconnecting with ordinary life after news of this kind, had not had an inspiration for Nandini's book choice. If Kamlesh had the time she was sure he would be willing to talk to them about the Taj though he was still working on it.

'Perfect,' said Nandini, 'he's a friend of yours, Rehana, please ask him. Frankly I'm ready for something romantic, some true love after all that Jennie business.'

Nandini ruled out Flowery Orange Pekoe. Men liked proper tea. And cake and sandwiches for a busy man, a diplomat who would be sparing them his valuable time.

Kamlesh said he would be glad to come and try out his perspective on their little group of discerning readers. He arrived with a few folded pages of his manuscript tucked into his trouser pocket and Aruna's notion of authorial airs and graces was quickly dispelled. Warmly welcomed and directed to the chair Nandini knew men liked, he began by telling them about his fascination for architecture because of the powerful feelings it could evoke. So he had been drawn to finding out what he could about that building of buildings, the Taj Mahal. It was built in the grand tradition of Mughal architecture, and like all their architecture it was massive, it was spectacular, it took your breath away just to stand and marvel at it from a distance. But this one was exceptional even for the Mughals, in its attention to the minutest detail. Contemporary Persian write-ups about the Taj waxed lyrical about its marble surfaces inlaid with floral designs and precious stones, the gold and silver that illuminated the tomb; the famed calligraphy of Amanat Khan on vast marble expanses of it, not to mention the size of the fortune spent on erecting it. An awe-struck Persian poet had written: 'Since the very moment of creation, who till now has seen an edifice like this?' And if all that wasn't exceptional enough, unlike any other building on earth it was a monument to married love and owed its existence to a bereaved Emperor's inconsolable sorrow.

'So,' said Kamlesh, 'It was that difference from all other buildings, its emotional aspect, that intrigued me.'

He smoothed his crumpled pages on his lap and read out what an agent of the East India Company, Peter Mundy, had had to say about it: 'The Kinge is now building a sepulcher for his late deceased Queen Tage Moholl, whome he dearely affected, having had by her nine or ten children and thought in her life tyme to use noe other women (which is strange if true considering their libertie in that kinde.) The buildinge is begun… Gold and silver esteemed common Metall, and Marble but as ordinarie stones…'

Kamlesh had to correct Peter Mundy. 'Mumtaz

Mahal had fourteen children in her nineteen years of marriage. Seven of them died and she herself died giving birth to the fourteenth.'

It was a tragic ending to a great love story, he said, but apart from that known fact, facts had been hard to come by. There were histories of Shah Jahan written by court historians because the Emperor wanted to go down in history, as his grandfather Babur had through his Turkish memoirs and his father Jahangir through his Persian memoirs. But the trouble with courtiers writing histories was that you drowned in their language. The Shah Jahan chronicles were so fulsome and flooded with praise of the Emperor's reign that you couldn't tell fact from fairytale: his 'sky-touching edifices, heart-pleasing gardens through which Hindustan has taken on immeasurable splendour, armies as numerous as the stars', and of course his noble character, his great benevolence and so on. The Empress was described as 'that holy-natured one of angelic character' and more such praise. And naturally no court history had anything to say about the private side of imperial life. But glimpses of it filtered into seventeenth century Europe through the tales carried by European travellers. These might well have been based on rumour and juicy court gossip of which there was no lack, but not entirely. There must have been something more substantial to go on. One widespread rumour that titillated Europe by the end of 1631, six months after Mumtaz Mahal's death, was of the Emperor's incestuous relations with their daughter, Jahanara.

'Yes, I know,' said Kamlesh, glancing up at the dismay he was facing, 'but we can't ignore it. Here's what the French traveller Bernier had to say,' and he read it out: 'The elder daughter of Chah-Jehan was very handsome, of lively parts, and passionately beloved by her father.'

'It was public knowledge that she was his favourite child,' said Kamlesh, 'and that her father had given her half the wealth left by her mother, and her six siblings had had to share the other half. As for the incest rumour, it must have been true. Bernier says the Emperor consulted the Mullahs about it: "Rumour has it that he rested on the decision of the Mullahs, or doctors of their law. According to them, it would have been unjust to deny the King the privilege of gathering fruit from the tree he had himself planted." So it seems the Mullahs actually gave him the go-ahead to sleep with his daughter. We can take it that it was true.' Kamlesh looked up again and said apologetically, 'Well, there it is. And apart from incest with Jahanara, there must have been plenty of gossip about his Majesty's morals for European travellers to be able to report it in such detail. According to the Italian, Manucci, the Emperor was known for the ways he indulged his sexual appetites "as if the only thing Shah Jahan cared for was the search for women to serve his pleasure," and that "his intimacy with the wives of his nobles was notorious." Manucci claimed he had authentic information: "I was admitted on familiar terms to this house, and I was deep in the confidence of the privileged ladies and eunuchs in her (the Empress's) service." He certainly left us what reads like an insider's account.'

Kamlesh went on to read it out: 'For the greater satisfaction of his lusts Shah Jahan ordered the erection of a large hall, twenty cubits long and eight cubits wide, adorned throughout with great mirrors. The gold alone cost fifteen millions of rupees, not including the enamel work and precious stones, of which no account was kept. On the ceiling of the said hall, between one mirror and another, were strips of gold richly ornamented with jewels. At the corners of the mirrors hung great clusters of pearls, and the walls were of jasper stone. All this expenditure was made so that he might obscenely observe himself and his favourite women.'

After more readings from European observers' accounts Kamlesh put down his papers and said,

'Well, I'm sorry but that's the way it seems to be. Maybe the truth lies somewhere between the court histories and the travellers' tales. But it's reasonable to assume that our inconsolable Emperor was not a one-woman man. How could he have been, with two other wives, hundreds in his harem, and the pick of whoever he fancied at court or in a crowd. Men who occupy thrones and have a free run are not known to be one-woman men. Witness our maharajas before they became ordinary citizens like the rest of us. Lechery has no religion.'

'All the same,' said Nandini, 'What a let-down. All those mirrors.'

'There are different sides to all of us,' Kamlesh offered by way of explanation to lighten the gloom, 'No one is all of a piece. They say Mussolini played hide-and-seek with his children and liked nothing better than to gather his family around the piano for sing-songs. Hitler was known to enjoy operetta, "The Student Prince",

"The Chocolate Soldier" and the rest. "The Merry Widow" was his favourite. For all we know he may have whirled his partners around to the "Merry Widow" waltz at Nazi merry-makings. Can't you just see him?'

They couldn't. The jolly side of Mussolini and Hitler did not make up for their disillusionment with Shah Jahan.

'When all is said and done,' said Kamlesh, 'There's really no doubt that Mumtaz Mahal was his true beloved. The palace and the entire realm knew it. It was the talk of the town. She even accompanied him to his battlefields. A legend like that doesn't spring out of nothing. Whatever he did in front of all those mirrors, with her he must have made love as love should be made. And after all, to end all doubt, there's the Taj Mahal.'

'Besides,' he continued, 'she was very much an ordinary mortal too, not the holy and angelic image of her in court histories.' He read what the well-informed Manucci had had to say about her less angelic side:

'Finding himself undisputed King of Hindustan, Shah Jahan was compelled to make war against the Portuguese of Hugli, for this was demanded by Queen Taj Mahal from whom the Portuguese had carried off two of her slave girls. He sent against them the general Qasim Khan who seized five thousand souls, among them some Augustinian and Jesuit fathers and carried them off to court. God willed that before they arrived there, the Queen Taj Mahal should die. There can be no doubt that in her lifetime she would have ordered the whole of them to be cut into pieces after great tortures. All the same, they did not escape a sufficient amount of suffering.'

After this final revelation there was nothing more to be said, so tea was poured.

'Someone should write about the women in harems,' said Kamlesh, accepting another slice of cake. 'There they were, captive for the rest of their lives. Hens in a coop being fed and fattened for roasting. Waiting for a summons that might never come. What do you suppose they did? Become lesbian lovers? Have hi-jinks with the eunuchs? Go crazy? Die of boredom? What women have had to go through is mindboggling. No wonder they've said enough is enough.'

After he had gone Lily declared, 'He's a real sweetie. What's his wife like?'

Rehana said they were separated. 'Gayatri is in the foreign service too. They kept being posted continents apart, and it was too much of a strain on their relationship. But they're on the best of terms.'

'Well, now let me show you my maternity creation,' said Lily.

She eased it out of its tissue wrapping, shook it delicately and held it up with the tips of her thumbs and forefingers. Their loud acclaim told Lily how exquisite it was. She pointed out its features—the silky softness and gossamer lightness of the fabric, so that its extra folds in front would hardly be felt on the growing belly bulge. Circularly cut, it curved gracefully from shoulder to ankle, its downward flow changing colour from violet to a glacial blue and ending in a fashionable uneven hemline.

They congratulated Lily on her inspired creation, saying sadists must have designed women's clothes through the ages. Fully clothed through her labour, Marie Antoinette had gasped and groaned behind a screen with the whole French court sitting on the other side chit-chatting while they waited for the newborn cry. It was the custom, to make sure the genuine royal article was being delivered and not a substitute smuggled in.

Lily folded her garment away. 'On the strength of this one, Mrs Ashwin is going to recommend me to her pregnant friends in Daughters of the Cultural Transformation. They're all pledged to five. I'll be making a fortune.'

'I hope you're going to take us out to lunch,' said Aruna.

'This deserves a cocktail celebration. I'll take us to the new Nirvana bar,' Lily promised.

~

The Rohners, back from their trip to the south, came to Rehana's to say goodbye, Kamlesh with them. He opened the bottle of champagne they had brought, a farewell gift from Nalin Ashwin. Arati hoped Gerda had shopped without a care because their excess baggage would be no problem. It would be flown to Mumbai in the Ashwins' private carrier and taken to the ship.

'It is a puzzle to me that readers do not understand the seriousness of my humour,' said Franz. 'Here is Nalin Ashwin making an honoured guest of me because he thinks my books about revolutions, including his favourite German one, are clever comedies when in fact they show the evil that men do in the name of revolution.'

They were full of their trip, Franz remarking on its architectural and historic splendours, and Gerda, ever the romantic, saying 'To stand on the tip of India is to be shocked by the sight of the ocean. What sight can compare with that for us land-locked people?'

Franz commiserated with Rehana about her father's disappeared books.

'The banning and burning of people, of books, how it repeats itself.'

He had persuaded the public library at home to open a wing for banned books. It was a great success, with books from the last hundred years. He wished her Papa's could have been added to it. Rehana could hardly contain her excitement. Nor could he when Abdul brought up the two leather suitcases and banged the dust off them. Franz and Gerda conferred in rapid German and Kamlesh was asked to go with Gerda to buy a new suitcase, but immediately, before the shops closed.

'It will be our excess baggage,' Franz told

Rehana while they waited, 'It will travel with us on our cruise and then home. I will stay in touch with you, Rehana.' He held out a hand and squeezed hers.

After the festivity of their champagne toasts to each other the room was very quiet.

Franz said, 'Your father's books must be preserved because he is telling how a civilization came to be, all that was happening in those times, the science, the music, the art, the intellectual life, the ordinary life in that long transition from ancient times.'

'But I suppose that was the trouble, Franz, and that's why they've been got rid of. There wasn't enough about the invasions. The Muslim invasions have been called the bloodiest in our history, some say the bloodiest in all history.'

Franz waved a dismissive hand. 'Can bloodshed then be measured? What we know for certain is there has been no shortage of it anywhere, and slaughters have surpassed each other everywhere. What is there to pick and choose between trampling a man to death under elephants' feet or disembowelling him alive? Or nailing six thousand rebels to crosses along the Appian Way as the Romans did? Or Hiroshima and Nagasaki? From far back until today it is a competition for who is the most barbaric and we have not seen the end of it.' It was his business to be in touch with ongoing atrocities for his researches.

What he had said made her tell him about the work she was doing, saying she had not realized she would be haunted by the images it left indelibly stamped on her. If only she could wipe them out, if only for a little while.

'This you can do, Rehana. Like the climber who grips every toehold on the cliffside, so must we learn to do. Enjoy the chocolate melting on your tongue, sing *La Vie En Rose*, walk among your Himalayan pines, and then there is fresh asparagus...'

She couldn't help laughing.

Kamlesh and Gerda came back jubilant with their find. The new suitcase was the largest and latest in elegant air travel. It had some room left after the books had been fitted into it. Gerda said she would lay her nighties and beachwear on top along with a copy of *Mein Kampf* just in case it was opened but of course it would not be opened on the Ashwins' private carrier.

When prolonged goodbyes had been said, Franz turned back from the car to add in his decisive manner, 'We will meet again.'

~

The Batlivala Gallery was a circular building facing the road. The courtyard had wrought-iron chairs and tables under garden umbrellas. Bougainvilleas were in exuberant bloom. Indoors there were cushioned chairs, no hard benches, for long and leisurely gazing, banishing the notion that a work of art is watched standing up and forward marching to the next one like a military manoeuvre. Seated, alone with the work, time stops. Then comes the illumined transporting moment that art bestows upon its gazers. Cyrus had hung the paintings far apart, each enshrined in its privileged space as befitted the celebrated art of a renaissance, each differently framed, uniquely itself and not just part of a 'movement'. Cyrus had been particular about that. Rehana surveyed the arrangement with satisfaction. She had told him she would stay back and look around the exhibition before joining him in his office. It was opening day when most viewers were likely to come. She felt nearer happiness than she had for a long time now that Papa's books were safely away and Nikhil's work was on view. She stood in front of one, reacquainting herself with it. Light flickered, flashed, leapt through deepening dark, expanding before her eyes into a lightning-lit landscape in the breath-held instant before the night sky explodes in a tumultuous storm.

She heard people arriving. A rock thudded past her ear into the stormy sky and crashed near her foot. She cried out as a knife pierced the landscape and stuck there. She turned in panic to see missiles flying straight as arrows to their mark. Something razor-sharp ripped through her sari. Something solid hit her head and sent her staggering to fall on shredded glass and splintered wood. Somewhere far away Cyrus was shouting through the din. Minutes later she felt herself being helped up, steered backward to the wall and lowered onto a sofa. Stunned and unable to lift her head she saw polished black patent leather shoes. A soothing voice spoke. 'Stay here, shrimati-ji, and you will come to no harm.' The shoes went away. The bombardment raged on. Raw pain stabbed one side of her and stung her swollen face. Her head throbbed. Her fingers came away wet with the blood on her cheek. Her uninjured eye made out gunny sacks in the rubble, empty of what they had carried. Thick dust hovered over battered frames, scissored canvases and broken furniture. The job completed, they piled their hammers, knives and shears back into their sacks and took their leave.

Cyrus had come to sit beside her. 'I phoned the police when it started,' he said, 'That was an hour ago. We must get you to a doctor.' Rehana gestured at the wreckage on the floor. 'All that later,' he said. Sitting speechless in his car she recalled the polished black shoes. No long white hooded robes, no high white pointed hats, no burning cross. It did not need a Klu Klux Klan to terrorize. Franz had said evil is an ordinary thing. Nice people, fond fathers, doting husbands do these things.

Cyrus had let Aruna know she would not be at their book get-together that week. There would be no book meeting, Aruna had assured him. All three of them came to see her, shocked by his account of the savage attack and the bandaged sight of her. Aruna had told her brother about it immediately and Hari, who worked under the DCT, had reported it to him.

'Hari says the DCT was terribly upset to hear what had happened to you.'

'Not to me,' Rehana spoke as best she could, 'I just happened to be in the line of fire.'

The DCT had expressed his sincere regret to Cyrus for the damage and the loss of his valuable property. Unfortunately, he said, national feeling once roused was hard to control. It had come to the notice of those men that the painters were Communists but they should have asked Mr Batlivala not to hold the exhibition, then this would not have happened. It was very reprehensible. Mr Batlivala must report it. The law would take its course.

'I know. Cyrus told me all that,' said Rehana, horror trapped like her voice and her tears behind bandaging.

'Rehana, it's no good being in the line of fire. You could have been killed,' Nandini was speaking urgently for all of them, 'As it is, the work you do is so depressing. Why do you have to be involved in things you can do nothing about?'

She didn't know why, unless it was hearing her mother say the unknown, unseen comradeship of other prisoners had kept her going, a hundred thousand of them in that last campaign not counting those who had been fined, flogged, or shot. How could they have borne it without the thought of each other?

'That's all very well but you mustn't go on with your work,' her friends insisted, 'Why did you get into it in the first place?'

Because people are tortured for refusing to agree the moon shines by day and the sun by night, because there are cells—hells—for the torture known as solitary confinement, because hanging doesn't break a neck, it cracks it and slowly strangles. And because of what happens up the road and around the corner. All this remained unsaid. They knew very well why she had started working with Asians Against Torture. It had started when she met the Indian group's founder at lunch at Kamlesh's house one day during the long emptiness after Vineet's death.

'But you take things too much to heart, Rehana. After all, what can you do about it?'

'We do what we can and it's little enough, even if it's only making public what people all over Asia including ourselves are going through.'

'Like what?' demanded Lily.

An instance out of daily hundreds across the sprawl of Asia, where warlords, ruling tyrants and madness ran amok, making free with human flesh? But she needed an example to convince them.

'In Uzbekistan,' she brought out finally, 'people who oppose Karimov get boiled in oil.'

They were aghast. 'It can't be. Not in this day and age.'

'And in Kazakhstan, Nazarbayev's torture chambers are just as fancy. We keep hoping other countries won't do business with them, but where there's all that oil and gas…' her voice trailed off.

In the violent world her work connected her with, whose actual acts of violence she had documented but not laid eyes on, she said her own accidental drubbing at the exhibition had at least given her a shadowy acquaintance with it. It was not what they wanted to hear. They got up to go, taking turns to put careful loving arms around her, and told her they would keep coming.

The bombardment came roaring back around Rehana. It had been as thorough as the razing of Guernica which had been cheerfully recorded as a rehearsal for the real thing. But here? What had brought matters to this pass? She brooded over the bombardment. There was not much else to do, immobilized and mummified as she was. Her sense of loss was searing. She had grown up in thrall to characters in books, on language that could desolate or exhilarate. She had discovered feelings she would not have known she had but for the beauty and power of paint. She remembered the first time she had heard the word 'painting' and thought it meant amazing. Nikhil was talking to her parents about his long-ago visit to Mexico where he had gone on holiday from university. He was recalling his sheer amazement. He had never seen paintings march across walls, move up and down huge high spaces, never known paintings could be stories inseparable from walls. The painter to whom he had an introduction was at the top of a wall-high ladder, at work where wall met ceiling.

As Nikhil told it: I am transfixed, looking up. My gaze is riveted to where intricate detail is holding its own undaunted by the sweep and size of the painted drama surrounding it. Finally the painter finishes and glances down. He puts his brush away and his bulky bulbous figure steps down the ladder, his back to me. Reaching the ground he turns around and his ugly face lights up, not at the sight of me, but when seeing me he exclaims 'India!' as if the sun has risen in all its glory around us. I am overwhelmed, not only because I am young and bedazzled in the presence of greatness, but because no other country has called an artist its most famous citizen, an artist whose wall paintings Mexicans trudge miles barefoot to see. Think Mexico and you think Diego. Think Mexico and you think art. I am at a loss for words but Diego Rivera is not. He is expecting me. The generosity of his welcome matches the breadth of his bulk, and it is not for me, an unknown Indian student but for the country I come from, where, as all the world knows, the most awesome reality is not the might of the British Viceroy or the guns of his King Emperor's occupying army but the man of whom Einstein has written: 'Generations to come, it may be, will scarce believe that such a one as this in flesh and blood walked upon this earth.' Think India and you think Gandhi.

Art is alive in the republic of Mexico. I am there at a time when artists meet, argue, quarrel. About real, surreal, abstract. Mural or easel? For the few or for the masses? Can art survive in Spain if the fascist Franco wins Spain? Has Lenin's revolution been bloodied and betrayed beyond repair by Stalin? Art is no reclusive ivory tower. It is passionate and political. In a struggle it takes sides. In this ambience, in such company, I hardly dare call myself an artist though that is what I know I am and the reason why I am here. Diego fans the flame in me. He points to the walls where he has painted two thousand years of Mexico's history from Aztec empire to Mexican Republic. It is all there, Aztec legends and splendours, Spain's barbarous conquest, the French and American invasions. All this is who we are, he says, and you have more thousand years for your walls. When I look puzzled about bestowing immortality on brute conquest, plunder and rape, he says it is our history so it is part of us. He points to the gringos on the wall and laughs. Where there is oil, he says, there comes the gringo! To me he commands: Go home and paint!

Would Nikhil's paintings have been saved, Rehana wondered, if he had painted murals? But once he was back home the fight for freedom had come first and jail took over. After that, undreamed of strokes on canvas took intoxicating flights from 'parampara' on the easel that served Nikhil as a wall, revealing us as creatures of our history. But wall or easel made no difference since the hardiest walls and highest mountains had not protected art. Machine guns had been trained on giant Buddhas in the Hindukush. Antique portals and pillars had been dynamited. Yet Franz insisted evil-doers are no different from the rest of us. They have brains, balls, veins like other men, no body part is missing, there is nothing you can single them out by. They are men who buy dolls for their children and light the candles on their birthday cakes. How do we know this, Rehana? In Nuremburg after the war, during trials of the men who had masterminded evils such as mankind had never seen, it surprised judges and onlookers that they looked, talked and behaved like ordinary men. This is how we know.

Catching up with her mail she found one from Franz saying Gerda had acquired a beautiful tan and on a 1920s dance night on the cruise they had learned to do the Bunny Hug. They had put on weight but did not regret it because the food had mocked abstemiousness and the Chinese had surpassed expectations. Out of the whole world's cuisine, Rehana, only the Chinese have excelled in the refined and subtle art of nuancing flavours. Nuance must be the secret at the heart of civilization. We in the West have lost the art.

Nandini came with grapes and cherries to speed her recovery and tactfully reminded Rehana to think about quitting Asians Against

Torture. A silent minute or so was usual now when talking was a bit of a strain, but Rehana's answer, when it came, only recalled the day she had first heard of it at Kamlesh's lunch. At the time, given Rehana's need for getting on with her life, Nandini admitted to the others afterwards, it had made sense. But it was doing her no good to go on with it. In casual conversation with a friend at the lunch that day Rehana had said the foreign service cut one off from the daily grind at home, diplomats were too far removed from it. The group's founder had interrupted tersely to assure her that we, here, were as far removed from what went on within shouting distance.

'Up the road or around the corner a man is being beaten bloody under interrogation,' he said. 'Another is stripped naked and kept standing naked for hours. Being dead at the end of it all is called suicide. And sexual savagery is everyday business. All this is news to you? That's what I mean.'

Loud laughter had burst out around them, a joke someone had told. Rehana could have joined in it herself. The repellant saga of treatment in police custody and the anger that had spelled it out had released her to a future she had forgotten existed, one that would occupy her usefully. In the beginning it had been no more than that. An opportunity came her way soon after when the group asked her to get the facts about a bicycle thief who had needlessly been kept in custody and only just released.

The garbage in the side street was no longer the mountain it had been. Sunk, scattered, spread, it was a stagnant stinking ocean in which skeletal cows and mangy dogs went fishing and ragged children dived diligently for pickings. The door of the dwelling opened an inch and another few inches to admit her sideways when she gave her name. A woman sat in a corner on the bare floor, knees drawn up, her arms hanging lifelessly over them. Her sari palla was pulled down over her face. A child lay on one of the two nivar cots. The haggard grey-faced man who had let Rehana in motioned her to the other sagging cot. Rehana sat down, unsure how to proceed. She had questions in mind and was ready to talk when he offered her tea, making a graceless interloper of her in the presence of timeless courtesy and putting him in charge in a curious reversal of their roles. Thanking him she declined and asked if she could talk to the person who had been released from custody. His eyes indicated the inert child and her questions were not needed. The man spoke: My boy took the bicycle from a public parking place. He is only twelve years old. It was just for a joyride. He left it somewhere further up the road where the police found it and returned it to its owner. That is all but the constable took him in. It was a hotel room the constable took him to, where he dragged his pants off, threw him across the bed and did the unspeakable upon his helpless body.

Her mind recoiled from the toneless clarity of his recital. The struggling child pinned down, his arms spread wide, a battalion astride him. In a futile attempt to shut out the image she took out her notebook and wrote down the father's and child's names. Mohammed Hamid and Jamal. We will do all we can, she promised. First a complaint would have to be made.

'No complaint can be made,' Mohammed Hamid informed her, recognizing a novice in these matters. 'They called a doctor to examine my boy. The doctor said there is no injury. Then he pointed to the constable and said to my boy, "Did this man torture you?"'

Rehana saw the constable standing, his legs immovable as tree trunks planted solidly apart, empowered by the authority of khaki, the child cowering. In answer to the doctor she could hear Jamal mumbling 'No'.

Mohammed Hanif's eyes were on her face.

He was making sure she had understood that fear was useful in resolving these cases.

~

Aruna was not going ahead with selecting a book for discussion. They were all still shaken by the bombardment on the exhibition and the thought that Rehana could have been killed. They took turns coming over to keep her company, and lavished their time, their work time, to help out with jobs that needed to be done. Rehana felt the familiar comfort of living off the soundness and normalcy of their lives as she always had, but now increased a hundredfold by all they were doing for her. Her godlessness, confirmed by what the human race was made to go through—no miracles of rescue forthcoming—had accustomed her to ruling out divine help. The miracle, as ever before in history, was human help and workaday human love.

Aruna brought avocados grown on a farm in her parliamentary constituency and some news. 'Hari says preparations are on for culture week. The Ashwins will be giving a party to announce it. You must come, Rehana, your bandages will be off by then and it's just as well to keep up with what's going on. Hari will send you an invitation. Lily says she isn't interested and Nandini won't be able to make it.'

But her first outing took her back to work, to the government office where the group had made an appointment for her. The government official looked up from the papers on his desk with an air of having been interrupted at work. Then, ah yes, Asians Against Torture is well respected. Fine work. He was sorry to have kept her waiting. Rehana said the organization wished to make an urgent plea on behalf of an asylum seeker beyond Afghanistan who faced certain death by beheading or by slower means if he was arrested. He was in hiding, awaiting word of permission to enter India.

The official looks grave and solicitous. Who does not value human life but asylum is a delicate, not merely a humanitarian issue, not a decision to be taken in haste, it takes time to ascertain credentials, who is this man?

He is a poet, an old man, and there is no time.

I understand, says the official, but we have diplomatic relations with his country, a region of strategic importance to us, not done to interfere in their internal affairs, would lead to serious political and economic consequences, can she guarantee this man is not engaged in subversive activity, treason takes many forms.

Rehana says he writes about hills, skies, meadows, of his love for his countryside. He reads his poems to his people. There are times and places where poetry gives heart and hope, the only hope.

Quite so, says the man at the desk that separates their consciences, but that is not the information we require, this being as I said a delicate matter.

'If he is captured they will do to him what they do to those whom they take prisoner,' she says.

With the detachment she has drilled herself in, she describes in short sentences the tortures in use upon body, mind and soul. The official's expression of startled disgust and acute discomfort makes it clear this degree of accuracy is hardly necessary. Most unpleasant if true. Much as we decry such treatment, if true, we cannot make an exception in his case without further investigation because if an exception is made in his case it will open the floodgates to asylum seekers. I do not have the authority to give you an immediate answer and we will study the report you have given us but I must urge you not to expect an answer in the near future owing to the factors we must consider in our relations with a friendly country as also the diplomatic correctness of the stand we take and now if you will excuse me I am already late for an official luncheon.

Out on the pavement she looked at her watch to begin the fearful vigil of counting the hours, twenty-four, forty-eight at most, until their thorough combing captured him. In times when economic consequences were more delicate than frail old skin and bone there was only one prayer. She closed her eyes and prayed. For beheading, not dismembering. For swift, not atrocious dragged-out death.

Her second outing a few days later was to Nandini's where they foregathered to talk about Aruna's book choice and life resumed its interrupted rhythm. Whatever was tearing the world apart, all loveliness last looked upon no longer there to see, here they could drink a tranquil cup of tea at peace in the enduring light of literature.

Aruna had chosen a novel just out about the despair of a lifetime condemned to filth removal.

He cannot wash his fingers clean of it nor scrape nor scour its abominable odours off his skin nor rid his nostrils of the foul inherited stench which is the curse of lifetimes that are spent skinning dead cows, handling human waste and living steeped in its filth. It is the malodorous breath he inhales, it circulates with his blood, it clogs his pores and lodges in the marrow of his bones. In desperation he seeks cure after cure and then is told the love of God will cure him. But having been unloved by God these past millenia he seeks the love of a goddess. Her bewitching young breasts, narrow thighs and beguiling slenderness receive and take possession of him. Ardour and appetite he has known but not the exquisite refinements of her five thousand-year-old embrace or such torrential surrenders to passion as at her lightest touch. When she eases him off herself he rises cleansed, purified, and liberated to live and breathe as other men do, touch and be touched like them.

Nandini said thankfully, 'A real love story at last.'

'An unreal one,' Aruna reminded them, 'Only a fantasy could free him of his occupation and give him a life of dignity. It's far from real.'

Rehana said, 'According to Picasso, art is a lie that makes us realize the truth.'

'Picasso didn't know us. The truth is this man couldn't have sex, much less a raging affair with a woman outside his stench-range. Nor could he decide on a filth-free life for himself. Even in the story he doesn't have a name. He's "he" all the way through. He's nobody and nothing. And caste makes sure he stays that way, forever untouchable.'

'Whether it could happen or not, I love the ending,' said Lily, 'He walks into Armani's and he's looking at jackets and a salesgirl comes up to him and says, "Can I help you, sir?" What a marvellous last line.'

They agreed it was a marvellous ending, one that only a writer of fiction could have dreamed up.

~

It was the Ashwins who sent a glittery invitation with an accompanying note on creamy monogrammed paper from Arati. They had heard. They were so sorry. She must come. Rehana decided to accept because it was time to be out and about. She dressed with a touch of frivolity for her return to the world in chiffon, gold bangles, gold sandals, and eye shadow.

Scotch was being served in squat square crystal glasses—a shape it was hard to get her hand around—in the velvet-curtained Persian-carpeted drawing room of the Ashwins' penthouse suite in their hotel. Champagne went by in crystal flutes, kababs and caviar on silver salvers. Arati Ashwin looked ravishing with Lily's creation billowing airily over her baby bump and around her girth. Lily was a genius. Rehana had expected the evening to have a formal tread about it, but ambassadors, movie stars, news anchors and other leading lights were standing around at their chatty intimate ease as if what the invitation had called a resurrection of national culture happened every day. It looked like a cozy family get-together. She stood at the edge of the party, clutching her square glass, hearing a man say killing the lover made it a 'crime passionel', not a crime.

Arati spotted her and led her into the gathering. 'You must meet Andy. His company has done the public relations for our event to put it on the map worldwide.'

Andy had the glow and affability of professional accomplishment. He and Nalin had been at Princeton together and this had been a most original assignment, spreading the word about a Hindu kingdom.

'Kingdom?'

'A slip of the tongue. That's what Nepal used to be. There are Christian, Buddhist and Muslim nations. Why not a Hindu one? The time is good and ripe for it. Definition is what it's about around the world. We specialize in policy makeovers.'

In answer to why it needed to be known worldwide, he replied, laughing, 'You don't exist if nobody knows you exist, and that's not as crazy as it sounds. Events have to get heard about. And PR gets practical results.'

Long before his time the company had done a job to boost Pinochet in Chile after his coup got rid of Allende. The results were there for all to see. Foreign capital rolled in, the economy boomed and there wasn't a thing you could buy in New York or Paris that you couldn't buy in Chile. Andy was twiddling the ice cubes in his Scotch on the rocks with one finger. She swallowed some of hers for its chloroforming effect, putting away the faceless bodies, scattered tongues and eyeballs of the disappeared in Pinochet's Chile.

'The company has done makeovers for celebrities too. President Carter's ratings went up when we got him to stop smiling. It made him look weak and undecided.'

In his polite American way Andy asked her what she did and Rehana explained. He looked politely sympathetic as over the death of a distant aunt for whom burial was the answer. It was his opinion there was no way around that problem. Not much could be done about it. Torture was here to stay like the arms race where it had to be weapon for weapon if you wanted to stay ahead. Power depended on it, on staying ahead of the competition whatever it took.

Arati took Andy away and Rehana went toward the beckoning arm near the bar across the room. Gaurav, dean of art critics, greeted her glumly, exchanging his empty glass for a full one.

'What's the matter, Gaurav?'

'The guidelines, what else? No breasts, no buttocks, no pubic hair, no abstract art. The word is holy art, healthy art, national art.' He helped himself dejectedly from a bowl of caviar. They had been given a preview of the entries selected for culture week.

'This too shall pass is what you're hoping, Rehana? Maybe so. Art may survive but judging by elsewhere, critics don't.' He signalled a passing waiter. 'Meanwhile there's caviar. Have some.'

'Who's the European in a sari talking to Nalin Ashwin?'

'Where have you been, Rehana? She's a German expert on womb science. She's written a book about Germany's remarkable rise after the two World Wars being due to the racial purification they went in for and the perfect Aryan specimens they produced. The DCT has invited her here to set up clinics like they had in Germany to produce pure Aryan babies. Right colour, right height, right measurements. Our very own master race, Indian style. The shastras and shlokas come into it. The position of the planets decides when to fuck and when not to. A darn sight fancier than the Nazi no-nonsense technique. Now that racial cleansing is under way with outsiders being ghettoed, Aryanization is taking a great leap forward. No, I'm not drunk.'

A stranger was approaching, his face and height distinctly familiar as he drew nearer. Seeing she was trying to place him, he said, 'We met at Franz Rohners' book launch. We were eating camembert. My name is Zamir. I heard about the exhibition. I was planning to go to it.'

She nodded, the memory of it constricting her throat.

'I heard you were there.'

She nodded dumbly again.

'Hari said you might need a lift home. I can give you a lift when you're ready to leave.'

She cleared her throat and said she was ready.

Zamir drove at snail's pace. His car crawled and stalled through the dark along their traffic-bound side of the road. On the clear side cars raced unobstructed. A hard-hit object hurtled across the divide. The glare of passing headlights shone on and off a corpse. The corpse stirred. Zamir got out to investigate, ignoring the cacophony of horns behind him as traffic lights changed. He picked up the mongrel and Rehana reached back to open the passenger door for him to lay the mangled body on the seat.

'She's alive but barely,' he said, driving on.

'What are you going to do with her?'

'Take her home and see what I can do. I'll take her to a vet tomorrow if she survives. But I'll drop you home first. I have to go much further on.'

'No,' said Rehana on an impulse, 'I'll come with you. You'll need help.' Very reluctantly he agreed.

She had no watch on and no idea of the time as they left the main road and drove on. It could have been midnight when they arrived. The stars looked down on a soundless world where nothing breathed. Lights were on in his house, left on, he said, to discourage break-ins. His arms were cradling the bitch and she was asked to get his house key out of his pocket and open the door. She fumbled with the heavy lock, finally turning the key in it. Inside, she followed his laconic instructions, fetching newspaper to lay the body on, watching him tie the hind leg hanging loose to a makeshift splint, handing him wet cloths soaked in antiseptic to clean and disinfect gashes in the dirty blood-matted hair, and finally a mug of water with a teaspoon to slide drops of it into the side of the mouth. Getting to his feet Zamir announced, 'That's all we can do'—the longest sentence spoken since they had entered the house—and went to the bathroom to wash his hands. Rehana stood holding the empty mug. She was gripped by a sense of powerlessness over things she could do nothing about. The mug slipped from her nerveless fingers and hit the floor with a clatter. Pain stung her jaw on its assaulted side. Knives glinted, flashing past. Iron split wood. Glass crashed and splintered under pounding feet. Sharp slivers of it raked her skin. Her legs gave way. She dropped into the chair behind her, hunched over and wept hysterically into her lap. When her frenzy wore down she sat up dazed and dishevelled. The room around her took blurred shape, slow to clear. It was calm, quiet, unravaged. A rolled carpet stood upended in a corner. Pictures waiting for walls lay stacked on bare floor alongside cloth piles folded wrong side out that must be curtains waiting to be hung. She drank the glass of water Zamir brought. He pulled her to her feet, leaned her briefly against him to steady her and said, 'Let's go.'

She found her gold mesh purse under her chair and followed him out. In the car she was assailed by smells of Dettol, Lifebuoy and wounded animal that clung to his clothes. At some stage of the drive home she recovered her tongue and was able to ask him why he had chosen to live at such a distance.

'I didn't choose. My landlord demanded my apartment back. He said the other tenants wanted me out and it was best for my safety as well as his own. No one would rent me another. Finally I had to move a long way out.'

She had a nagging need to ask him something important and kept trying to remember what it was. Giving up, she asked if they could meet one day soon. Zamir said he would be in touch.

Franz wrote back in answer to her last mail, sounding elated about culture week and the paintings selected for it. From the point of view of his researches, it was bracing news. It fitted perfectly into his study of revolutions. Had he not said they repeat each other ad infinitum, imitate and echo each other? She must let him know if this culture week would also have a parade because the Third Reich's culture had been launched with a five-mile parade. A procession of knights in armour, Valkyries and Rhine maidens was followed by the Wehrmacht marching in magnificent precision. The soldiers of the SS brought up the rear in the famous black uniforms of their awesome corps. Franz had a diary in his possession describing it. The diarist, Erich, had been there on that July afternoon in 1939. A day of national pride, Erich had noted. Munich was gaily decorated and the whole city had turned out to watch the parade. The Fuhrer himself was there watching it for the entire two and a half hours. For Erich it had been a thrilling emotional experience.

'What you say of your stormtroopers' fury,' wrote Franz, 'how familiar that, too, is. Like at the Batlivala gallery, all the masterpieces of modern art were cleared out of German museums and healthy art was hung in the new House of German Art: peasants ploughing German soil, happy German families, heroes of Greek mythology dressed up like Hitler Youth in brown shorts and black belts. But unlike your guidelines there were nudes, male and female anatomies of the purest Aryan proportions. It is said the Fuhrer stood admiring the Swan raping Leda and bought it for his own collection. In case you don't know this Greek myth, Rehana, it is Zeus disguised as a swan who rapes Leda. But the painting that rejoiced the Fuhrer had a Wagnerian Swan about to rape a German maiden.'

Franz was relieved to know her face had mended except for the barest scars, her eye could open wide and her other wounds had healed. As for the destruction of Nikhil's and all the modern masterpieces, the deepest mourning would not be deep enough. As in nature, it is the prelude. First the skies darken, then comes the storm. Trees know it is coming when their leaves start to shiver.

'In times like these, Rehana, marvels like duck l'orange, the spy sagas of Le Carre, and *C'est si Bon* on the immortal Satchmo's trumpet, are gifts sent to us to assuage our grief.'

To these gifts Rehana could have added 'the

glimmer of moonbeams through iron grating for the prisoner on her jail cot.'

The post brought contracts from Franz for her to sign and return. He had found a publisher for two of her father's books.

~

The telephone beside his bed rang. Kamlesh picked it up on the first ring. Calls at unearthly hours of the night were Gayatri's, this time not for one of her work-related chats or nuggets of news passed on for his interest or enjoyment. She sounded urgent. She was upset and alarmed by the news. Was it true? Why was his book being junked? Was he in trouble? Should she consult a lawyer about it? The last question was a quintessentially Gayatri reaction.

'What in heaven's name would a lawyer in Peru know about censorship in India?' he said in late-night exasperation.

'Let me tell you, Kris,'—an abbreviation she had coined that had no connection with his name—'there is nothing this continent doesn't know about censorship, crackdowns, invasions, coups and assassinations. This continent has been through it all. How else could they have produced such amazing writers?'

Gayatri's immersion into the past and present of wherever she was posted was legendary. It made her brilliant at her work.

'So, what's happening about your book, Kris?'

'All I know is someone on an investigating committee rang my publisher and asked him questions about me. Sudhir is going to tell me about it at lunch tomorrow.'

'Then I'll ring again tomorrow night.'

Universal Books specialized in history and politics. Sudhir had had a healthy respect for Kamlesh since they had published his *Genie* two years ago. The title notwithstanding, and in Sudhir's opinion its starry-eyed view of the Non-

Aligned Movement, the book had apparently brought recent history alive for its inheritors. Sales had been consistently high. Their association had ripened into a warmth beyond business matters.

'They don't want it said they are banning books, so they are just disappearing them,' he told Kamlesh when they were seated at his Kashmir Club, 'like inconvenient people were disappeared in Chile and Argentina and other places and only their bones were left to tell the tale. But as books have no bones there's nothing left to prove they were there. Anyway, don't let that spoil our lunch.'

Sudhir, a strict non-vegetarian, proceeded to order kabargah, dum kaleji and shaljam salan with rumali rotis, and a bit of vegetable on the side.

'The man who came to see me wanted to know your political affiliations.'

'I don't have any,' said Kamlesh.

'He says your praise of non-alignment shows your political affiliations.'

'It's ridiculous. The book is about the end of empires, the birth of nations, and a huge change in how the world was run.'

Sudhir had brought a copy of *Genie* with him. He handed it to Kamlesh across the table. 'I've highlighted the parts that are causing trouble.'

Kamlesh flipped through it and came to a highlighted passage. He read it aloud: 'Hardly had one war ended when another had begun with wartime's victorious allies now sworn enemies divided by an arms race against each other. Better had the atom not been split, and the power to annihilate millions with a single bomb never been placed in human hands.'

'And further on you are weeping for the Japanese people,' said Sudhir.

'People don't want wars. They don't make wars. They only get killed in them. And the atom bomb was not the end of the story. After the war they tested their H-bomb on Bikini, never mind the people who lived on the island. There was never a greater need for non-alignment. I've said so.'

'I know. It makes you out to be a pacifist,' said Sudhir playing devil's advocate, 'and that's not allowed nowadays.'

'It was never allowed. Anti-war campaigners are dangerous bloody nuisances. Locking them up has always been policy. But I'm not a pacifist.'

'I believe you, but these investigators ferret out what suits them and make what they like out of it. They are saying you were against the Vietnam war when you were a student and you marched in an anti-war procession.'

'Of course I did. I happened to be in Calcutta and I joined in and shouted "amar nam, tomar nam, Vietnam" with all the rest.'

Sudhir enjoyed that recollection. A meal that had looked enormous to Kamlesh was, to his surprise, getting steadily eaten while they talked. Outrage stimulated appetite.

'As you say, Kamlesh, being anti-war has always been dangerous. But now, my friend, it's blasphemous. Your investigator says war has the sanction of our scripture. It's the plot of our sacred books. It's what they are about. Opposing war makes you sacrilegious along with the fact that your book is a security risk now when we are threatened. I forgot to ask him by whom.'

Over steaming fragrant kahwa Sudhir warned, 'The man may call on you. I am more sorry than I can say about the book, Kamlesh. Apart from anything else, it means big returns gone down the drain. We could have fought for it on any other ground but charges of blasphemy and national security make it impossible.'

'It's a good thing I don't have to earn my living by writing,' said Kamlesh.

He repeated the conversation to Gayatri when she rang that night.

'What you make a living by is the next thing they will go after,' she warned. 'That's the well-known sequence.'

'In the Peruvian lawyer's opinion no doubt. But we're not Peru, Gayatri. For God's sake, we've grown up in freedom. This is India.'

Queer how those three words had a liberating effect.

'You know, Kris, you've had your head buried in Shah Jahan's incest and his other shenanigans. You haven't noticed what's going on around you or believed it's for real. Please keep in mind what my Peruvian friend says. I tell you these people have known all about such matters since their Incan empire.'

Gayatri's opinions came of her own colourful reasoning. Regardless of the Peruvian lawyer and Peru's tormented history Kamlesh fell sound asleep.

In his office a few days later he got up and stood at the window. It was what he often did when composing reports, stare out of the window until words came. This afternoon none came. His mind revolted at the thought of submitting to the death of his career. No investigator had come to see him as Sudhir had warned, only a letter informing him he had two choices. He could resign from the service with immediate effect or be summoned for an official enquiry. In other times sacrilege had faced an Inquisition that burned heretics at the stake. The charges against him would 'detain' him behind bars for no known length of time. The country had to be protected from the danger of peace.

His father had joined the foreign service at its creation after independence and Kamlesh had grown up on talk of beginnings. A new nation, flag, anthem. A republic proclaimed, its foundations laid on ideas that became the nation's meaning. There had been the grouses and grumbles of a newborn service that was poor and powerless, unversed in power-play, and up against hoary wielders of power, yet had made its voice heard in its own vocabulary: West Asia instead of Middle East, Asian, not Asiatic, Muslim, not

Moslem, and other more significant corrections to the skewed perceptions set down in history as indisputable. It had taken stamina and sly humour to insist on being oneself. When an irate Dulles barked, 'Once and for all, are you with us or against us?' Nehru replied, 'Yes.' When a roomful of power-wielders demanded, 'What is your country doing about population control?' they were told about the woman seeking foolproof contraception and her doctor prescribing a glass of water. 'Is that all, doctor? Before or after?' and the doctor saying, 'Instead, Madam, instead.' Laughter brim-filling the room. What other way was there to remind the powerful, the prosperous, the arrived, what they had forgotten about the pains of arrival?

They tell us there's nothing new under the sun but that's not true, Kamlesh's father had said, we trod new ground. We blazed a trail: no taking sides with warring Powers, no joining their wars, no giving them bases to bomb others from, no truck with war. It's peace we're after. Now, thought Kamlesh, we're in the race for bigger, better, deadlier. His inquisitors were right about his book. The pursuit of peace violated holy writ.

The letter of resignation he knew he must write came to him, page after page of strongly worded, reasoned, seasoned argument. He went back to his desk, sat down and rubbished it all. Explanations were for prisoners in the dock. His anger dictated one precise sentence. He wrote it with a Parker pen in thick black ink on official stationery, had it delivered, and sat on at his desk. His palms felt clammy on its familiar ink-stained surface, his fingers traced its dents and scars. His closed eyes summoned the angles and corners of the room he knew by heart. The best of his knowledge, experience and ideals had found expression at this desk, in this room. It was not the last time he would be in it. He would have to come again to clear up, but never again would he be here as of right. He had not imagined that losing the work he had given his life to would be so devastating. Regret, heartbreak, desolation welled up in him.

At home he immersed himself in Shah Jahan, concentrating on completing a book that might not see the light. Sudhir had cautioned it would be wise to wait until the furore died down and his name got crossed off the inquisitors' Most Wanted list. These things blow over. Now that he had resigned, he would be forgotten. Be that as it may, a book once begun and long lived with could not be left unfinished. Kamlesh got on with it. The Taj love story had had the most dismal of endings, with the lover who built it dying ill, old and wretched, imprisoned in the Akbarabad fort. Kamlesh decided on a livelier ending for his book. He found the grande finale he needed in a contemporary account of Jahanara's extravagant grief for her father/lover describing her as 'The precious pearl of the casket of chastity, (who with) the other respected ones of the holy precincts of fortune and honour, turned their rose-coloured faces into blue-hued ones through blows and slaps of grief, shedding oceans and oceans of lustrous pearls on the earth from the oysters of their eyes…'

Gayatri rang to say her assignment in Peru had come to an end and she would be coming back soon. No news or ministry gossip had reached her about where she was likely to be posted next. She would stay with her sister till she found a place of her own.

The Taj story completed and put away, Kamlesh was able to come out of his book-imposed cloister and ask Gayatri's sister for news of her arrival. He made a note of the date, airline, flight and time and told Malti he would meet Gayatri at the airport and drop her off, it would be no trouble. Malti gratefully accepted his offer. She dreaded having to cope with parking, luggage, flight delays and other airport miseries.

The plane was on time. Gayatri came out of

the terminal, caught sight of Kamlesh and stayed rooted where she was, unrecognizably mute and stricken. Something was inconceivably wrong. Illness, disaster, worse. Ice touched the pit of his stomach. Grim possibilities closed in on him. Fear propelled him forward. Gayatri flung her arms around him and clung to him crying 'Oh Kris, what have they done to you?' Hardly daring to breathe his arms tightened fiercely around the long-lost cherished feel of her. It did not seem possible they had ever been parted.

'Where to?' he asked, starting the car.

Still shaken but with a ghost of her sparkle, she said, 'Home, of course, Kris. I'll ring Malti from home.'

Malti received the news of their change in living arrangements with outer matter-of-factness and vast inner relief. She had almost given up hope of their seeing the light.

~

Cocktails at the Nirvana bar had been long postponed but at last a date could be agreed upon and they were there, Gayatri with them. The bar was seductively low-lit and designed for intimacy. A waiter stood nearby, looking past them.

'Funny how he doesn't see five of us,' said Lily. 'D'you suppose he's waiting for the men of the party to arrive?'

She lifted an arm for his attention, which he saw and raised his own hand as if to say he'd seen.

'I'll have to go and collar him,' said Lily, when they saw a man crossing the room, coming towards their table. He and Gayatri greeted each other with delight, kissing each other on both cheeks after which she introduced her friend, Carlos, the Cuban ambassador. The ambassador sketched a salute in graceful acknowledgement of their smiles and took in the four new faces with evident admiration. It was a far cry from the meaningless gallantries that social graces seemed to require and which they despised. The ambassador was clearly a man to be cultivated.

'Join us, do,' urged Lily, backed by her companions.

Alas, he had to decline as he was just leaving. Some friends from home were coming to dinner to celebrate Fidel's survival of the CIA's forty-fifth attempt to assassinate him.

'They never give up, do they?' said Gayatri.

Their own delayed tribute to Lily's enhanced income owing to the new Nazi policy of permanent pregnancy seemed unworthy in comparison. Instead of joining them which he would have been happy to do, Carlos asked their permission to order a celebratory Cuban cocktail for them to toast Fidel. The waiter came with full speed. Daiquiris were ordered and paid for and Carlos said a heartfelt goodbye. He would have stayed but for Fidel's and his country's continuing good fortune.

They toasted Fidel in all solemnity but the

heady Cuban cocktail and the reason for it had a sobering effect. Fresh from South America, Gayatri said, 'These things happen to them all the time. They're geared for the worst. We go on saying it can't happen here. Being India will protect us, as Kris kept thinking, even when the signs were clear as day. Fancy Kris, an experienced observer like him, not realizing what was coming to him.'

Rehana sensed an unspoken belated agreement amongst Gayatri's four listeners that they had been wrong and fiction had got it right. Kamlesh, like the manor in Rehana's book choice, had not noticed the centipedal slither of things to come. A reminder that but for art, we would never know thc truth.

The waiter came to remove their empty glasses and place five more daiquiris before them.

'We didn't order more,' protested Lily, and was informed that the gentleman had placed a double order.

'Well, to Fidel again and Cuba,' said Gayatri, picking up her glass and clinking theirs.

~

Gangu was off duty and Rehana was in the kitchen cooking. Kamlesh's description of his meaty lunch with his publisher had put her in mind of her Nani's incomparable koftas. Abdul watched her fingers blend oil and curd, masalas and hingh into the mince. He was standing by ready to chop and slice as he did to help Gangu and was looking on in fascination. No onion, no garlic, then how meat?

Rehana introduced him to the secret of hingh. He watched her make sausage shapes of the mince in the palm of one hand and deliver them delicately to ghee and curd in the frying pan. He was an eager learner, taking the pan from Rehana and moving the koftas around with care. He asked if he could use one of the suitcases that had held her father's books for his own belongings and give the other one to his friend Suraj who worked in his father's shop of kitchen utensils in the market. Suraj could come and collect it after eight o'clock when his father closed the shop. Rehana knew Dhiru's shop, invitingly stocked with stainless steel and shining brass.

She worked late after dinner finishing a report for the group with her favourite ghazals as background music to keep out traffic and night noises, but all was peace and stillness when the music stopped and her work was done. She walked out into a moonlit brilliance that had the caressing mildness of late spring, the gentle interlude between winter and the harsh heat to come. The garden slept. Its fragrances floated up to receive her gratitude. She strolled out to the far end of the lane where the old flowerpot vendor lived under his tarpaulin shelter and stored his gamlas, displaying them on the main road for buyers when morning came. He was awake, sitting huddled and half hidden. On the ground opposite him the shock of a human mound held her rigid. At sight of her the old man gabbled, beseeching help. Eight of them came, she kept hearing, would come back if they had seen him, if they knew he had seen four of them tear the clothes off the boy, force him to his knees, swing their rods high and then down to break his back and crack his skull, shouting what leather is this, is this suitcase made of cowhide as if the dead can answer. Bright moonlight burnished the skin torn off the blood-reddened back. Greyish slime oozed from the split skull. Rehana had heard him and Abdul clowning in the kitchen while she was having her dinner.

Everything in her ground to a halt yet her brain worked, informing her this was no clumsy haphazard killing. Four had surrounded him. What of the other four? They had watched, memorizing which blows where and how many. The mathematics of it had been tried, practised and perfected somewhere else, and somewhere else before that. The act of killing had been fined down to a repeatable reliable recipe. It did what a single bullet or a spray of bullets could not do. Alive one minute, dead the next, was not the purpose. It was the interval in between that punished.

Rehana found herself on her knees beside the body, as paralyzed as he had been, confronted by deadly danger. She felt the terror of being encircled by weapons poised to strike, the helplessness of skin and spine against the savagery to come. Feeling went no further. In the unbridgeable chasm between herself and the sufferer, between one person and another, her flesh could not feel, nor ever know the agony his flesh had endured. She willed herself upright, straightened her buckling knees and walked back to do what had to be done. Suraj's body, Suraj's father, the police. At some hour of what remained of the night she said a requiem for the faith of her fathers. Sanatan dharma had been slaughtered in cold blood this night.

The group took charge. She would not have known what to do. She didn't know hierarchy had the last word in death as in life. An empty field outside city limits had to be found for the cremation, the sticks and twigs and fallen branches collected by them augmented by logs purloined from a place they knew, a makeshift platform awkwardly constructed. No priest, no prayer, only themselves and Dhiru, made of stone, beside them. Stone cannot light a fire. Someone had to. She took the lighted stick handed to her and did as she was told, stepping back as the wood kindled and a wisp of smoke began its spiral into the darkening sky.

The next day they found the utensils shop had been ransacked. It was expected, the group told her, for selling kitchenware that caste Hindus would cook their food in and eat out of, a man ordained to skin dead cattle, lift roadside garbage and high-caste shit, pretending to be what he wasn't and thinking he could get away with it. Ungrateful, these chamaars, though they were allowed to sell the skin and bones and other body parts of the carcasses they skinned. Dhiru had disappeared.

The police reported a body found mysteriously dead.

~

Zamir arrived unexpectedly. In the effort of carrying on Rehana had forgotten she had asked him to come. He said he had taken a chance and dropped in without warning as he found he had a free morning. Free from what? She knew nothing about him. He was a stranger she had met twice before. Conversation had hardly figured in their acquaintance, and their last meeting had ended in her uncontrollable breakdown. She now remembered why she had asked to meet him again. It was where he lived, at a safe distance from the eyes and ears of the city's centre. That, and something to do with his personality, the deliberate way he had gone about rescuing the mongrel, ignoring the cacophony of car horns behind him and getting on with what had to be done. The poor creature had died, he told her. She must have been past saving when he rescued her.

The lawn was damp from watering. They stood on the verandah, she wondering how to ask a favour of him when he went down the steps to the wet grass to look at Abdul's flowerbeds, and then in comic bewilderment at her, making her smile. After a puzzled second—making sure she actually knew how to?—he smiled warmly back, came up the steps and sat down. The reason for his visit was slipping from her. She called it back, remembering why she had wanted to meet him again. It was where he lived, at a safe distance from here, and the need to find work and shelter for Hanif, the boy Cyrus had rescued from the ghetto, and his mother. She explained the vital reason for it. Would it be possible for them to work and live somewhere out there? Zamir thought about it. For a tailor there was sure to be work. About Hanif he was less certain until Abdul came out with guava juice and Zamir was reminded he had not yet found household help. If Hanif would work for him, Zamir would make sure he had time to paint. This unexpected solution and the enormous relief of it took Rehana unawares. When she collected herself and thanked him it was with an intensity that made him ask if she was responsible for their safety.

'No. Yes,' she replied, not bothering to elaborate.

It was a long time since she had felt so much herself in a masculine presence and exactly like this never before, a feeling she did not put down entirely to his having seen her break down for no apparent reason that night, but rather because he hadn't asked her why. It was a habit he apparently had of ignoring what came in the way of getting on with what had to be done which dispensed with the need for explanation. However, one does not sit saying nothing when one's guest is occupying the other chair on the verandah and conversation is supposed to be made which was what she was not doing.

A brief peaceful silence later he said, 'I would have come sooner but I had visitors.'

His doorbell had rung. He had answered it. Men walked in. One sat down, the others stood. They were deputed to collect books for neighbourhood book-burning fiestas. His was on their list. They had come for it. The standing men parted to let him through. He brought his copies and handed them over. Rehana's immediate shock came of hearing he had written a book.

His latest novel, he said, *Unholy Love*. Rehana sat up, her shock complete. The stark unfolding of the tale and her admiration for it was as vivid as the day she had read it but the despair of a lifetime spent removing filth was by someone else. She heard Zamir say it was his pseudonym, no longer a protection. She was appalled. Could he be serious? Huge ancient megaliths and mountainsides had not withstood religious wrath, what hope was there for a pseudonym? The week-ago night returned, the murder of Suraj securely welded to crimes past and to come. What crimes? Bodies had been found mysteriously dead. She asked Zamir what he was going to do. The men had told him this was a warning. He was sitting with his long legs stretched out, his hands resting on the arms of the garden chair, his eyes on the flurry of a flight of sparrows from a low-hanging branch of the cassia.

His novel, a horror story made luminous in the telling had affected and enchanted her as nothing had in recent literature. But knowing a novel was not knowing the writer, there seldom being a congruence between the two. She waited for what she knew he was going to say, 'I must get out, go away somewhere so that I can write in safety.' He turned to look at her and said instead, 'I must get started on a new novel' and then, 'Can I take you out to lunch?'

They lunched at home, the longest lunch in recent times. Rehana talked of what was uppermost in her mind, his novel and its unbelievable happy ending. Zamir agreed with her emphatically. It was a most unlikely ending and not one he had written. The character had chosen it. Set characters down on a page and they take over, as when dance takes over the dancer, and song the singer, or when a swimmer high-dives in an arc of its own volition and not the swimmer's. Or when a woodcutter's axe becomes a rhythm that takes over. The illustrations were endless, he said. Rehana listened, attracted by his workmanlike illustrations. She understood what he was saying, but would anyone ever understand the mystery, the sorcery, of that transforming moment? Talk extended over coffee and after, shared talk about shared passions.

That night she woke with a start and reached for her bedside lamp. His arm was there before hers, switching it on. The moon outside her window was seven days thinner, waning ritually, indifferently as if it had not lit up an orgy of blood and brain seven days ago. She turned and wound her arms around Zamir in a strangling grip, pushing her face against his chest for deliverance from the sight, repeating, 'I can't go on with it, I won't go on with it.' It was a decision she made from time to time.

Next afternoon she was at the site with her group, looking down, forcing her gaze downward on naked buttocks branded with a swastika. Another body branded Om across torn breasts, stared up at her. A pregnant belly had been sliced open, the pulp that had been a foetus plucked out and tossed aside. Legs lay wrenched apart, metal rods inserted. Smoke was rising from the smouldering flesh of a neatly constructed human pyramid. Rehana stood soldered to the ground. The ghetto Hanif had escaped had crumbled. Fires raged among the ruins. Her companions were picking their way through bodies intertwined in death by arms, legs and heads flung over each other, looking for a sign or a flicker of life. The group's founder was making a tour, counting corpses, two hundred and fifty female and as many or more butchered males. He was speaking to the policemen on duty, asking how. Who knows but it is said an explosion caused by a leaking cylinder had set the tenement on fire, Rehana heard a policeman say. So careless, these people. We have been sent for to collect the bodies for burial. There will be no delay, the graves are ready, dug deep for mass burial. She recalled Cyrus telling her the DCT was in charge of racial purity and the ghetto came under his watch.

At the DCT's office they were cordially received and invited to sit in a semi-circle in front of the shining expanse of his desk. The purpose of their visit? Ah yes, the fire. He listened gravely, saying he was aware of the unfortunate incident, he had received a full report, and he understood their concern. But however regretful, this is not a matter for your group, my friends, an accidental fire caused by carelessness as so often happens.

Rehana sat forward in her chair, speaking succinctly for the group, stating it was torture they had come about, the butchery, the branding, the mutilation. Well aware that the words had grown sterile with repetition and no longer shocked whoever heard or read them, she had made it a practice to describe the result in each such case in precise detail. A solemn silence from the DCT who inclined his head, waiting for more, his hands clasped loosely on his desk. Well then she would give him more. She had no proof, only her profound inner conviction backed by knowledge gained from Franz, for what she said next. It was a case of arson, she declared. It was one of the uniformed tribe who had set fire to the building. The tribe itself had come armed with Stone Age and newer weapons, prepared to massacre. The mass graves dug beforehand to speed disposal gave her announcement absolute authority.

The DCT's face cleared as though all was now understood. His hands unclasped and spread wide in appeal. If what you say is true, my friends, even should that be the case, then is it not natural? Should our people not get carried away remembering our history? Is it not reasonable that they should do to our tormentors what our tormentors did to us? And now, my friends, let me offer you my cardamom tea. Its fragrance is unrivalled among teas.

~

One day a wild wind blew through life on earth, wrote Franz to Rehana with his typical flourish. You have seen what wild winds do, whip branches bare of flower and foliage, and so with those that sweep nations, as this extract from Erich's journal shows. I am sending it to you for a reason I will come to after you have read it. But first, here is what Erich writes in his journal:

> There comes a point in life when there is no turning back. For me it came as I watched the parade in Munich that July day of 1939. It was a parade of our culture, from the classical to the present time when we are a military Power like none other ever before and the magnificent marching figures of the Wehrmacht and the SS displayed our military might. The SS soldiers were unique. The insignia on their black uniforms looked like strokes of lightning above daggers and death's head badges, a uniform that sets them apart as the Party's own soldiers, to deal with its enemies. But they are also chosen for their racial purity. Herr Himmler who is Reichsfuhrer of the SS in charge of national

security and racial purity is known to oversee the selection process himself which screens candidates for the weight, height, and bodily proportions by which an Aryan is known, and it is Herr Himmler who set up the training years ago that hardens their minds and prepares them for the tasks they have been chosen to perform. I knew as I watched the procession go past that it was the career for me. I had the Nordic features, the hair colour, eye colour and physique for it. That day it became my ambition to serve in the SS.

How am I to put into words my excitement at being selected and to learn we are handpicked to carry out the national policy of increasing the numbers of the racially pure. The Fuhrer's slogan 'Europe today, tomorrow the world!' forsees a future ruled by a master race of surpassing fitness. Survival of the fittest is common knowledge—the Fuhrer has called it 'the iron law of nature'—yet who but he has had the genius to apply this law of nature to the human species of the white race to evolve what Nietzsche called Ubermensch, a superman who will be as superior to ordinary mortals as men are to apes. This dream we are called upon to serve is the religion of the Third Reich.

Clinics have been set up for Lebensborn, this 'fountain of life' experiment that is new to humankind. There we bring blue-eyed blonde German women—golden blonde, butter blonde, silver blonde—and mate with them. Women are also brought from Norway that is now occupied by us. We do our part. It is an act to be efficiently performed, ramming through resistance to achieve results. There is no question of sexual pleasure given or taken, though there is no lack of sexual pleasure in our lives. Thrilled by our victories in war, enthralled by our uniform, inspired by the spirit of the times, women go with us for the asking. The Lebensborn clinics are for the science of eugenics. The body under you

> enclosing your member is there for penetration and impregnation. The larger programme for racial purification and racial hygiene sterilizes or exterminates sub-humans. These are the Jews and the weak and useless people among us as well as those in the countries we have occupied.

That is what this diarist writes but he does not say what became of the pregnant women or the children born of the Third Reich's religious fervour. The women gave birth in secret in Lebensborn homes and were sent back to wherever they came from. Their racially pure offspring were put into special orphanages or given to Nazi couples to bring up, and were christened in a sacred ritual with an SS dagger held over the infant while the foster mother swore to uphold the Nazi ideology. Those that were born disabled or defective, or later became so, were killed or sent for extermination to concentration camps.

Can this be true, how can it be, you must be asking as you read this, Rehana. It is a question we keep asking and others after us will keep asking though it was all revealed at the Nuremberg trials. There are realities that imagination cannot conceive of and will not allow, making us cling to how can it be.

So this is the family matter I told you I was writing about because I myself and Gerda were conceived in Lebensborn clinics by unknown Erichs of the SS. Our unknown mothers gave birth in one of the twenty Lebensborn homes in Germany and Norway. At our christenings under SS daggers our foster mothers swore allegiance to the Nazi religion, and we would have grown up to become the next generation of the master race if in our infancy the war had not cut short the next thousand years of the Reich. Instead we grew up, myself here and Gerda in Norway, reviled, abused and hated as offspring of Nazi eugenics, to discover each other years later. This was at a meeting of other Lebensborn offspring trying to find some comfort in each other in our shameful common predicament. Imagine that you are looking into a mirror, only it is not a mirror but another person in a roomful of other persons who like mirrors are reflecting and repeating you. No, it was not quite like that, it never could be exactly that, but the attempt had thrown up likenesses, those unlike having been eliminated at the start.

Thank God, you will say, that what I have been calling revolutions or transformations or by whatever name they choose to call themselves do not all go so far. Yet they do, if not to manufacture racially pure anatomies then to manufacture minds that mirror each other's so that you do not know your thought from another's because they are the same thought. Why else the purges and massacres if not to purge us of the danger of thinking differently? Think like me or face extermination. On and on they will go, Rehana, until exterminators realize we are born to be different from one another, nature has made us so. I once saw a carpet I was told was handmade true Persian which is what I wanted as a gift for Gerda. On careful examination I found its design was exactly similar along all its borders and all through its entire length and breadth as only a machine-made product can be. In handcrafting there will be at least a shadow of a fault, which is the mark of a human hand and its claim to authenticity. But we will talk of all this when we meet soon because Gerda and I have accepted the invitation of Nalin Ashwin to come for the culture week and we shall be there for the grand opening. Speaking as a writer, it will give me the ending for my new book on my family matter, though it gives me no pleasure that the disastrous link between you and us is now established beyond doubt and the past of my country has become the future of yours. Have I not said all revolutions, transformations, or call them what you may, follow the trodden path?

~

Rehana wondered at the most remarkable days of her life going by unremarked, already a habit. Zamir, helped by Hanif and Hanif's mother, unrolled carpets, hung curtains, placed furniture, books and possessions where day by day they would acquire the permanence they had lost in transit. A city's breadth away she carried out the jobs she was assigned in the campaign against torture and its cult of human sacrifice, covering her face with her hands against unbearable recurring images. There was no interruption in either life, both prizing the continuity essential for work. The wind blowing across the nation was left to blow while they grounded themselves afresh in their occupations, his to write, hers to act on behalf of. The time they spent apart was a renewal of resolve, time together a land of discovery. They were lovers who knew what lovers know, that no love is carved in the image of other loves. It is itself, forsaking all others. Fortune had favoured them by accident or chance. Neither of them believed in fate, so their meeting being destined was out of the question, leaving each of them secretly wondering what else it could be.

The question arose whether Rehana should accept the DCT's invitation to the gala opening of culture week. He was evidently still mindful of her drubbing and making up for it. Admit two, the invitation said, unnecessarily since Zamir baulked at missing precious hours of a whole morning's work. But Franz's impending arrival decided her and persuaded Zamir. Franz was looking forward to winding up his book with this climactic event on the path to cultural transformation. It would mark the announcement of Hindu nationhood, the Anno Domini from whence the new era would date, all else relegated to BCT. As always, it was following the well-established pattern. Our past is your future, he had written to Rehana.

~

The early summer day already felt hot on bare arms but the opening ceremony was to be under a shamiana on the spacious gracious lawn of the Directorate of Cultural Transformation's glass and steel high-rise. It was not yet the blistering heat that would wither the panorama of rose-red flowerbeds and the blush-pink beauties draping the garden wall. Astrologers had picked the day for its auspiciousness, but it could well have been picked with an eye for the lawn's lush greenness and the fragrance of flowers in bloom that a hotter sun would extinguish. It was still the season though fast approaching its end, for silk saris and kameezes adorned with a fashionable abundance of costume jewellery, dangling earrings, wristloads of bracelets, beringed fingers and the spangle and jangle of beads. The occasion demanded high fashion and cameras were poised for it as the shamiana filled with invited guests who had no premonition of, or preparation for the cow carcass on the rambler roses, its fore- and hind legs splayed rigidly on either side of the garden wall. An evil-smelling carcass landed near the shamiana, screams came from the shamiana as another descended on a flowerbed, burying it under the stench and fumes of putrefaction. A slight breeze lifted and wafted the fumes above and around. Under the canopy Rehana held down blowing strands of her contaminated hair and wiped her watering eyes. The lawn, a battlefield of stinking sunlit corpses in grotesque postures of rigor mortis, had no trees to obstruct the coming and going of their carriers. Rehana had the strange sensation of not believing what she was seeing, this declaration that Dalits would leave dead cows to rot: Here they are, all yours. Skin and chop them for disposal yourselves, it's not our job any more. Absurdly she looked for Dhiru in the tumult. Had he joined his outcaste comrades in their ultimatum to caste? How had they dared when lynch mobs roamed highways and byways in daylight and moonlight, skinning and slicing those they called cow thieves, cow traders, cow eaters, cow insulters?

The shamiana was a den of panic and suffocation, no way out of it. In its befouled smothering confinement a woman retched violently and vomited. Someone fainted.

Zamir pushed his way out, negotiating a track between carcasses, avoiding collision with rigid upright limbs or hind legs flung rigidly apart. Over the wall he saw corpse-filled trucks. Fifteen truckloads of decaying cows were taking time to offload. The road was in an uproar, shots being fired, police at war with truckers. No rules of warfare were being observed.

Rehana coughed and choked where she sat in a suffocating stupor, nauseous in the fumes. She reached for Zamir's hand, not there, his chair empty, no shoulder to lean on. She had an overwhelming desire to lean on his shoulder. She was aware of legs shuffling past, the shamiana slowly emptying, Zamir back and urging her to get up but first she had to tell him there was a sublime justice to it, this memorial of a kind to Suraj, the beauty and the poetry of this Dalit revolt. Zamir pulled her up as he had done that night and held her against him, this time in the passionate embrace of lovers in a perfumed paradise.

~

Three hours later at a table for six in the dining room of the Ashwin Hotel, menus lay unopened before them and napkins unfolded. The maitre d' hovered, muttering sotto voce. The city, the country, in shock—who could have foreseen and what now? He held his hand to his forehead as a Catholic would have made the sign of the cross and went away leaving them, he thought, to study their menus, but in reality to wonder at the morning. Left to themselves Franz admitted that his theory that all cultural transformations proceed along the same hallowed imitative path would have to be altered in his last paragraph. There were variations. Some proceed from below. It would seem we have here this exception. He would have to rewrite his ending. He looked around the table to encourage opinions.

Zamir said, 'As you see, endings have a way of writing themselves, as in novels.'

'Not so in politics,' Franz pointed out.

'Except at times when politics becomes poetry,' put in Kamlesh, 'as it has again and again,' and he gave examples. Gandhi. Rosa Parks. Mandela. Poetry had come from a prison cell in Nehru's words, 'Who lives if India dies? Who dies if India lives?' and at the stroke of a midnight to mark a tryst with destiny.

'But a novel has also given us darkness at noon,' said Franz. 'No poetry in that famous darkness. But yes, it seems there are exceptions.'

'Like this morning,' said Rehana.

The spectacle returned to astound them with its size and scale. Shackles had never been cast off at one blow. No ultimatum had been so astoundingly choreographed. The experienced researcher in Franz welcomed this dramatic unexpected conclusion to his manuscript, but for fear of subduing the rejoicing around the table he refrained from saying the end is not yet. In the days ahead there would be much work for Rehana and her group. He put on his glasses and picked up his menu, holding it open between him and Gerda. She put it firmly down.

Thought-reading is well-known to married couples. Gerda said reprovingly, 'All that may be so, Franz, but do you forget we are together to be joyful ? Where is the wine?'

The wine ordered, Franz picked up his menu again while the others, talking animatedly among themselves, seemed content to leave the choice of food to a connoisseur. This morning was proof to them the tide had turned, the monster of religious rule and holy war had been averted and all would be well. Franz did not know whether to weep or to marvel at such innocence in the face of all the evidence since time began. Instead he turned the pages of his menu to soups. Looking around the table he enquired, 'Shall we have vichyssoise to start with or,' turning another page, 'shall we start with shrimp?'

Acknowledgements

The extracts dated August 13, 1942 to August 22, 1942 from a prison diary are taken from the diary kept by my mother, Vijaya Lakshmi Pandit, during her third imprisonment, in Naini Central Jail, Allahabad during 1942-43. It was published by The Signet Press, Calcutta in 1946 under the title *Prison Days*.

The foreign travellers' views of Shah Jahan are taken from *Taj Mahal: The Illumined Tomb*, compiled by W.E. Begley and Z.A. Desai, published by The Aga Khan Program for Islamic Architecture, 1989.

THE FATE OF BUTTERFLIES

Prabhakar, returning home one evening, comes upon a corpse at a crossroads, naked but for the skullcap on his head. Days later, he listens to Katerina's stark retelling of a gang rape in a village, as chilling as only the account of a victim can be. And in a macabre sequence, he finds his favourite dhaba no longer serves gular kebabs and rumali roti, while Bonjour, the fine dining restaurant run by a gay couple, has been vandalised by goons.

Casting a long shadow over it all is Mirajkar, the 'Master Mind', brilliant policy maker and political theorist, who is determined to rid the country of all elements alien to its culture—as he, and his partymen, perceive it.

A professor of political science, Prabhakar observes these occurrences with deepening concern. Is the theory he put forth in his book—that it is not the influence of those who preach goodness and compassion that prevails, but the matter-of-factness of cruelty—playing out before him?

In the midst of all this, he meets Katerina, beautiful, half-Russian, wearing the scars of a brutal incident as a badge of honour. Together, they discover that, even in times that are grim, there is joy to be had.

There may be trouble ahead,
But while there's moonlight and music
and love and romance,
Let's face the music and dance.
Before the fiddlers have fled,
Before they ask us to pay the bill, and while we still have
    that chance,
Let's face the music and dance.

—From the film, *Follow the Fleet,* 1936

He sat at a table near the window looking down on the blue and purple cluster of potted hydrangeas at the entrance, and beyond the pavement puddles to the rain-drenched monsoon light of the August morning. A steam bath outdoors but air-conditioned to pleasant coolness in the restaurant, not to an Arctic freeze. He was comfortable in cotton. Bamboo-framed watercolours of flowers and foliage by French artists brought a European springtime to the room. The wall-hanging opposite had a Tree of Life in blossom, delicately hand-painted in rose, cream and crimson dyes. Its original had been designed, he had been told by the owners, for the flower-loving Mughal emperor, Shah Jahan.

Bonjour was a breakfast retreat he had discovered on his previous visit to Delhi six months ago, and breakfast was being served. Not his hotel buffet with something for all comers from smoked salmon to items labelled idlis and parathas, here it was served on order, à la carte, granting respectful attention to the day's first meal in recognition of a day that for many of its patrons would demand every ounce of concentration, and if negotiating minds were not already made up, skilled persuasion. Tables were spaced to allow conversation that neither intruded nor was overheard by others. He felt he was back in a civilized era before noise became endemic.

Coffee was a treat. It came, as before, in the common clay 'kulhar' in which, he had been told, tea had always been served by tea vendors at railway stations and roadside stalls but had now been discarded in favour of dingy cups and mugs. He dissolved a teaspoon of brown sugar crystals in his coffee, stirred it, and took a meditative sip. It had never had this earthy richness or aroma drunk out of china. Francois and Prahlad, the couple who owned Bonjour, clearly had a genius for combining the best of both their worlds, the one French, the other Indian. Prahlad saw him and smiled. He walked over, stepping with the nimble grace of the dancer he had been, rested a hand on Sergei's shoulder by way of welcome and went on his way, leaving Sergei to order and eat in peace. He ordered Eggs Benedict. The menu informed him that hollandaise sauce on poached eggs had been thought up in the kitchen of New York's Delmonico restaurant, and was not as he had fancifully supposed, a creation of the Benedictine order of monks whose spiritual ardour had not interfered with their taste buds if the liqueur named after them was any indication.

Two breakfasters at a table near him were foreigners like himself, but young black-haired men. They had their briefcases with them, presumably going straight on to their business appointments, and a file open between them, conferring while they ate. They looked fresh out of courses in markets and management and as focused as any samurai on their targets—unlike himself who at their age had been reluctantly weaned from the classics and a desire to write, to be trained for the future his father had so resolutely built. But that apart, the young men belonged, like him, to the tribe of frequent travellers for whom travel meant flying visits and distance had no literal meaning, with any country an hour or a night's flight away. A far cry from the plodding journeys of centuries past, on foot or mule or camel, on wheels or sea-craft at the whim of sea winds, by traders risking the perils of travel to peddle their wares. An unlikely beginning it had been to the saga of seizure, occupation and empire that trade became. The old *Punch* cartoon showing Cecil Rhodes triumphantly astride Africa from Cairo to the Cape with a rifle slung over his shoulder, told the story. A fascinating subject, the story of trade.

His own business had been completed yesterday. The discussion had gone over the ground covered six months ago with some major additions, and had confirmed the decisions taken. The same senior civil servant, worthy successor to the steel frame that had administered British India, had chaired it with professional ability. A disappearing breed, he had heard it said. There had been two other men present, one of them apparently an official whose specialized knowledge was needed for final purchase orders. The other man had been introduced, but vaguely. Sergei had not caught his designation but his presence seemed to be more than that of a trustworthy aide required to sit in and report. The hint of deference towards him implied something more. Either way, an extra presence was usually the sign of a new political dispensation.

The meeting had taken place in the same room as last time but Sergei had noticed changes. A decorative display of swords and daggers with handles of intricate elaborate craftsmanship and shining sharp-edged blades adorned one wall, and were obviously collectors' items chosen by weapons enthusiasts. And entirely different portraits commanded the wall space above the sofas. New founding fathers? He was reminded of his father's bleak joke from Soviet times, with one nervous apparatchik asking another, 'Let me know Who's still Who.' It also took his mind back to a side street in a Lusaka backwater where a poster painter kept posters of rival politicians stacked for sale because 'You never know.' Sergei had been amused and impressed by this gem of street wisdom and the man's grasp of the way things were. Quick change was the name of the game when power changed hands overnight as in coups and sudden takeovers, and during post-imperial slugfests for control in shaky national situations, but a clean sweep of founding fathers was the last thing he would have expected in the democracy that was the republic of India.

For Sergei it had become a matter of observation, not opinion, a cardinal rule of commerce being its distance from politics, but political riddles of this sort were intriguing.

'We only make use of the opportunities politics provides,' his father had made abundantly clear, and there had been plenty of those during the Cold War, like the upheaval in Indonesia that overthrew Sukarno in 1967.

'The new regime under Suharto swung into action right away disposing of Communists,' Dimitri had told him, and lest his son and future heir have misgivings about the manner of it and demand to know why—the kind of question Dimitri had asked himself in a time gone by and knew it had no answer—he had tutored Sergei in the workings of power: 'There will always be those who call the shots and those who bear the brunt—not our concern.' He had added, with the detachment that accounted for his success in the manufacture and sale of armaments, that all sides had profited from the Communist bloodbath. It had earned Suharto America's pleasure and brought billions of dollars into Indonesia's petroleum industry. President Ford and his secretary of state, Henry Kissinger, had enjoyed a cordial dinner with Suharto and given him carte blanche to invade and occupy East Timor. This he did the day after the dinner party, first thing in the morning. Dimitri recalled the massive military operation that had needed the most advanced weaponry from him and other suppliers.

Sergei knew his father for the complex character he was, too discerning a mind to be boxed into the crude either/or of the Cold War. He knew Dimitri had no love for either side. He had been a Communist and true believer until Stalin's show trials and purges forced him to flee with his knowhow and his secrets into exile, escaping the single blinding light, the inquisitor's dark shape at the desk, and certain death. His commitment to the cause he had served had died instead. If the grandeur of Lenin's vision had been so treacherously and blithely sabotaged, if Trotsky, its last surviving hope, was later hunted and murdered in far-off Mexico, then what chance had any dream, or the dreamer, of survival? Robbed of the faith he had lived by and with no place on earth he could think of as home, he had built his second life on his past experience with support from the French who had given him asylum.

'Alfred Nobel was very upset when a French newspaper called him "a merchant of death" for having invented dynamite,' he told his son, 'The newspaper described him as a man who had "found ways to kill more people faster than ever before," and so Nobel got himself remembered for prizes instead of armaments, including a peace prize. But many another roaring trade has as much and more to answer for, Sergei. Cotton was grown by slaves. Slaves planted cane and made sugar out of it. Slaves extracted rubber and got their hands and feet chopped off if they didn't produce the right amount, and diamond miners were stripped to check them for hidden diamonds and got their hands cut off if they were caught stealing. You could say trade of all kinds has blood on its hands. And then there are children working on plantations—it's cheaper.

'As for the sanctity of human life, Sergei, who remembers Bikini was where the H-bomb, which was equal to twenty-nine thousand A-bombs, was exploded, now that it's a wisp of sexy swimwear? Or that Lumumba was killed for winning an election that Belgium wanted him to lose, and wasn't the name of a Congolese cocktail? But shake up milk and cocoa, add cognac and pour it over ice cubes—in the world we live in, that's a Lumumba.'

Sergei, Paris-born and British-bred, had inherited a going concern complete with his father's handed-down access to those who mattered. Otherwise, except for his fluent Russian, inheritance was missing. Not so much as a stray snapshot had survived the flight from the homeland. Nothing either to inspire or offend. It was a strange situation he had come to accept. No remembered sight, smell or taste had been bequeathed to him in a deliberate burial of memory. His mother had talked yearningly of the life they had left behind but she had died in a car collision, though in reality of exile, when he was a child. His father, abruptly widowered, had no reason left to look back, memories being of no use to a survivor who had no one to share them with. Dimitri lived intensely in the present he had carved out for survival. Sergei wondered what he would have made of the swords and daggers, and the new founding fathers. He was finishing his breakfast when Prahlad joined him.

'How long are you staying this time, Sergei?'

Longer, he said, to give himself time to relax and look around. Prahlad patted his hand approvingly and said he hoped this didn't mean only monuments and museums.

'Don't forget we're here, too, Sergei! You must meet a dear friend of ours. And I will be dancing for a special occasion. You must come.'

Back at the hotel Sergei found an invitation from

the American ambassador to dine at the embassy the following evening.

Books had their unexpected ways of getting started. This one had begun when Prabhakar turned his car into the driveway, not noticing the new name on the gate.

The young woman looked up as the car drove in. Cars were not supposed to come in. The gate was kept closed so that no child could run out on the road. But there it was in the porch with someone getting out of it and surveying the scene.

Prabhakar saw the young woman getting up from where she sat on a durrie on the grass among small and very small children. Two or three of the smallest jumped up too. It was a pretty picture, the young woman surrounded by children, and it had a familiar ageless charm. It got him idly wondering why some images stick and others fade. What was it that made some images and ideas live on and become the bedrock of our beliefs and values? He walked up to her.

'Can you tell me where I can find him?' he asked, giving his friend's name after greeting her.

He had been away for some time and he didn't know the house had changed hands, or that it had become a school, he said. She disentangled a child's grip on her sari and shook her head.

'The house is not a school. It belongs to a friend who lets us use the garden for our nursery school. It's for two-to-six-year-olds. There are the verandahs and that big sheltered terrace for when it rains,' she told him, 'We run it ourselves. Parents take turns. The three of us are parents.'

She waved a hand behind her. Two women her sort of age were supervising the activities of boys and girls with a notable lack of supervision. One or two were getting no help clumsily pushing coloured wooden beads onto a cord. Older ones were plastering sheets of paper with randomly chosen colours from their paintboxes and some were chalking unrecognizable squiggles all over a blackboard. A few were sitting at a long low stone table drinking juice. He noticed the juice was being drunk out of glasses, not disposable paper cups.

The table was covered with a starched white cloth and laid, to his astonishment, with peony-patterned porcelain china.

'We give them lunch before they go home,' the young woman explained, and seeing him staring at the table, 'This is how we get them used to beautiful things and to handling them with care. You'd be surprised how careful children can be. The glasses and china belong to our friend who owns the house.'

A joyful shriek from the infant at her side made her bend down swiftly to prise open his fist. The crushed butterfly fluttered faintly and lay still. Another feeble flutter of its papery purple wings, and then to her evident relief, it flitted upward and away.

She looked up at Prabhakar in indignant appeal. 'Can you believe some schools teach children to collect butterflies and kill them? Did you know butterflies get thirsty and like to settle on wet leaves for drops of water?'

He didn't know and he was ready to leave but she was still talking.

'It's easy then to catch them in nets and kill them.

There's a horribly cruel technique to it. First you have to squeeze the poor thing through its middle to cripple it and then put it in a jar with some acid stuff for a couple of hours. That's how long it takes to be sure it's dead. After that you take it out and stick a pin through its middle and frame it in the same frame with all the other butterflies you've killed. Is that the way to teach children about nature?'

'I mustn't keep you from your work ...'

That's quite all right and would he like to know more about the school, she asked? Prabhakar was about to decline, tactfully, so as not to hurt her feelings. He was impatient to be on his way, and would have taken his leave if the ghost of an idea had not crossed his mind. He stayed.

'We feel parents should be connected with their children's education right from the start,' she was explaining in her earnest fashion, 'That's why we don't have teachers teaching them at this early age. We don't believe in telling them what to do and making them memorize things. We want them to use their own minds and to experiment. Art and handicrafting are good ways to begin to do that, don't you think? Besides,' she continued anxiously, 'we want them to respect living things and be sensitive to their surroundings. We want them to grow up to be caring and kind and …,' she thought hard for the right word, and settled for 'well, good, kind people.'

And the opposite of all that had got the book started and finished in record time.

Dinner at the American embassy was informal. Sergei knew no one except his hosts, the Judsons. The other five guests were Indian and seemed to be on first name terms with each other. One husband was a known name in the media, another in ruby and sapphire mining. Over bourbon and bonhomie the talk was animated and cheerfully political, everyone agreeing that things had never been better.

Jake Judson explained the good cheer to Sergei. The new regime had brought in major changes. Opened up. Taken sides with the right people. Got off the fence at long last.

'They've got real,' Jake summed it up with vigour, 'You can see they mean business. You can see the adrenalin flowing. The change has been a long time coming. How did your meeting go?'

It had gone excellently, Sergei told him. But how about these major changes that everyone was agreeing about? 'Did you pick your guests so there'd be no arguments to spoil dinner?'

Jake laughed heartily, 'Nothing like that. Ask Linda. She picked the guests. These are the people who enjoy her down-home Southern cooking. Lindy thinks the world needs educating about the South. She's from an old Virginia family. Confederate folks. Incidentally, you don't have to drink Jack Daniels. You can have Scotch if you prefer. Lindy won't hold it against you.'

Sergei said the bourbon was welcome, and held up his glass to salute Lindy across the room. She blew him a kiss in return.

'Tell me about the major changes, Jake.'

Jake said he would get Kritik—'He's the bright guy who edits an influential weekly'—to put Sergei in the picture over dinner, but his own reading was that the warrior caste had taken over, they being number two in the caste hierarchy. 'You could give them the credit for the turnaround in policy and the business-like way they are getting things done. It takes a military mind to get down to brass tacks.'

At dinner pulled pork took the place of major changes. 'Why is it called pulled pork, Lindy?' from one of the wives. 'Because it has to be cooked real slow in a heavy pot for hours until it gets so tender and juicy, you can pull it apart. This is a Louisiana recipe.' It was agreed that no meat had ever tasted as succulent. Unheard of accompaniments called sweet potato casserole, Southern creamed peas and buttermilk biscuits upheld the pork's high standard and Dixie pie was greeted with acclaim. A mellow company moved to the drawing room for coffee and brandy. No one was in a hurry to leave. Major changes were forgotten.

'How's the family?' Lindy asked Sergei.

His son was working in the New York office, he told her, and his daughter had just had a baby. Susan was revelling in grandmotherhood. He and

Susan were getting on so much better since they had separated.

'That's so true, isn't it?' remarked Lindy of separations and divorces, and then of marriage, 'The first time you marry is a trial run, like the first waffle. You have to discard it.'

Back at his hotel Sergei rang his daughter. It was the right time for London. 'How are you, darling? Are you all right? How's the baby?'

'We're both fine, Daddy, don't worry, and she's the sweetest. You'll love her. I'm breastfeeding her. On demand , not by the clock, so I'm up at all hours but it's good for both of us.'

Sergei worried about Irina—named after his mother—about her health, her happiness and above all, her politics. Of his two children she was the one he worried about. Slight, soft-voiced and slenderly built, Irina looked appealingly feminine and vulnerable. The contrast could not have been greater with the views she held dear, and activities of the kind that were much better left alone. He was hoping motherhood would change all that.

'Are you enjoying your time off, Daddy? What have you been doing?'

'I've been eating Louisiana cooking. Pulled pork and Dixie pie.'

'But I thought you were in India.'

'I am. This was at the American embassy.'

'Oh no!' in dire dismay, 'How could you? After they invaded Iraq for oil they had no right to, and Vietnam before that and the atom bomb before that. And the gun lobby in full swing over there.'

'But it was a good dinner.'

She laughed. She hadn't mentioned his own arms-dealing and never did. Sergei knew this was not out of any concern for his feelings but because of her conviction that 'People have to realize for themselves. It's no good shoving ideas down their throats.'

'Anyway, Daddy,' she said, 'think of a name for the baby. A beautiful name.'

He promised he would think of one soon.

During a sabbatical from teaching, Prabhakar had taken a break from political science and written a lighthearted book about the why and how of societal changes with a chapter on changing fashions in clothes. The idea had caught his fancy on a flight from Delhi to Mumbai, flipping through a lavishly illustrated fashion magazine that had been left on the seat beside him and reading that women's wear had radically changed during the French Revolution. It had been liberated from imprisoning corsets and innumerable voluminous petticoats. Change is what fashion does, but what had brought about an inside-out makeover as dramatic as this? Exploring the period he came to the conclusion that the fashion revolution had nothing to do with the great Revolution's liberty, equality or democracy. It had happened because American cotton cloth and English (though really Indian) cloth was flooding the French market. Cotton in all its weaves and variations, from fine to finer to weightless and transparent, was all the rage in France.

Prabhakar, freed from the classroom, had let his imagination take over. It must have been the first time since Grecian antiquity that a garment had been allowed to flow down a woman's body with no hooks or wires or stiffening, no bulk or coarse fabric to impede its flow. Gauzy muslins revealed glimpses of the long-barricaded, suffocated feminine form in all its allure and desirability as nature had designed it. Hair got liberated too. No more rigid styling, it was no longer rolled, crimped, powdered or wigged, just gathered into the most casual of buns that a touch would unloosen to spill out.

Prabhakar pictured Josephine and her women friends clad in the blissful heady freedom of cotton in her salon at Malmaison among admirers and would-be lovers. With intimacy within hand's easy reach, seduction had never been so effortless, and what could be more natural now that Josephine's most infatuated lover—her husband—was away conquering Europe. Was it her infidelity that had led to her dismissal from Napoleon's bed and would she have remained his adored mistress even after he divorced her to marry royalty but for the cotton that had flooded Europe?

And so to the next question. Would the French

market have been flooded with foreign cotton and French women so enticingly robed but for slave labour in America and England's rapacious plunder of India? The personal and the political thus, as always, inextricably entwined. French fashion's romance with cotton had lasted until Napoleon banned its import to encourage France's own silk manufacture, but Prabhakar had not been able to resist adding the teaser: And who knows why else Napoleon banned cotton, making way again for corsets and petticoats and iron control of women's bodies.

Reviewers had shrugged off Prabhakar's humorous take on societal change. Entertaining but. A bit beyond poetic licence, or, if there was such a thing, academic licence. And to what purpose? What was the point of taking liberties with history?

'I'm not the first to do it,' said Prabhakar, but his interviewer had not heard of the hilarious English classic, *1066 and All That.*

Prabhakar took time to explain. It was his conviction that the personal and the political were inseparable. Private matters, even the most intimate, could make a decisive difference to the course of history. Think about it, Napoleon might have won the Battle of Waterloo and Europe's future would have gone on being Napoleonic for who knows how long if it hadn't been for his haemorrhoids. He had a terrible attack of haemorrhoids on the morning of the battle and had not been able to get on horseback to inspect the battleground, so he couldn't plan, as he always did, the course of battle. It was a fatal omission. The interviewer said it was a good story but history was not about what might-have-been. Prabhakar persisted. Political events—whether they made history or not—had to be seen in terms of human beings, the men and women who took part in them. You had to make room for personality and even for bowels—like Martin Luther's chronic constipation. The sixteenth-century German professor of theology, who later became a priest and monk, had spent hours sitting on his toilet seat. That's where visitors met him. It was where ideas came to him. Sitting on that stone potty he wrote his famous ninety-five heresies challenging the Catholic church. The fact is the Protestant Reformation was born out of Luther's chronic constipation.

The expression on the interviewer's face implied: What next in outlandish examples? But Prabhakar carried on, saying what's more, you could never leave out the unexpectedness of the human spirit.

'Such as?'

Such as ... but it was a poem his friend Rahman who taught literature had read to him that came to mind. Trapped in the hell of trench warfare the English poet had not written, as you might expect, about his dread of his head being blown off any minute, but of laughter, peace and gentleness—those were the words in the poem—and of himself as 'a body of England's, breathing English air, Washed by the rivers, blessed by suns of home ...'

Prabhakar was a popular (not yet full) professor, known for taking his students on journeys beyond the text, and his book had delighted those who were familiar with his mix of politics with its human side. There had been enjoyable exchanges about it in and outside class.

Back to teaching, he had not given the subject

of societal change another thought until the day of the nursery school in the garden. It had got him wondering what made an idea like kindness or compassion (even for a butterfly) become a mark of civilized behaviour. How had it happened that in times indifferent to suffering there had appeared men who were obsessed with the suffering of others? A prince had renounced princedom in his lifelong search of a cure for it. A prisoner in the agony of crucifixion had prayed for his torturers: 'Father forgive them.' An emperor wept after victory in war, appalled by the carnage, and vowed never to make war again. Men who were out of the ordinary. In a world without pity, in the savagery of their times, they had envisaged another world and made a religion of compassion.

He had intended to write a new book about the lasting impact of these men, but another narrative had written itself, the truth being that their impact had not been lasting.

On the other hand, the everlasting indifference to suffering was vividly documented and in great detail. He did not need invention or imagination to describe it, as he had in his word-play about the pleasures of promiscuity in muslin. What baffled was the matter-of-factness of cruelty. A man had thought nothing of hammering nails through the living flesh of another man's hand. A man had operated the rack that stretched another man's joints beyond human endurance a fraction at a time. Practice had perfected and refined techniques. The terror of men and women delivered alive to ravenous beasts in the Roman arena had been popular entertainment. It was not hard to picture the Romans who thronged the terraces getting an afternoon's thrill from the spectacle of human flesh in animal jaws. All this had happened and gone on happening in its infinite imaginative variety.

Specifically, his narrative had taken the turn it did because driving home from the nursery school that day, he had had to lurch sideways and brake violently to avoid running over a body that had suffered the fate of butterflies, but bloodily axed, not pinned, through its middle. It lay spreadeagled on the road, naked but for the skullcap on its head, with the axe left propped against its side, two signatures announcing: This is why and this is how. Was this a sign of things to come for those whose faith was Islam? Prabhakar had fallen forward on the steering wheel and lost track of time. When he straightened up, drizzle was spattering the windscreen, blurring vision. He got the wipers going and started the car. By the time he reached a crossing, rain was slamming the roof of his car. He had to shout through the window to the traffic policeman who said, yes, yes, we know, we will be removing it, and waved him on.

His book was out. Classes had resumed after a short break. He had driven to the university, past the tank at the entrance, its turret pointed at entrants. It had become a fixture he hardly noticed any more. His classroom was half empty, holiday lag quite likely. He had started to speak when a girl in T shirt and jeans stood up in the back row and screamed, 'How could you? How could you write a book like that?' and was gone before he could say he would talk to her later.

'A brilliant book,' the vice chancellor said, stopping him in the corridor after class, 'Extremely well put, the point you make. I congratulate you.'

Prabhakar acknowledged the compliment warily. The new—now some months old—vice chancellor was the one who had requested the tank, to instil spine into the students. The VC turned around at the end of the corridor and called, 'Can you look in tomorrow morning for a few minutes? My office, at ten?'

Prabhakar raised a hand in assent.

Someone was with the VC in his office next morning. He had come with a letter for Prabhakar and been told to bring back a verbal reply. To save time, the VC explained. Prabhakar opened the letter and read the few lines from, good God surely not, the eminence whom he and one or two of his colleagues called the Master Mind, the man who was head of the regime's policy-making cell, inviting him to his house tomorrow at four: '...people you will be interested in meeting in view of your book ...' Ten seconds, twelve, were long enough to read the brief note. He sat saying nothing for much longer. The VC and the official messenger were in amiable chit-chat. Prabhakar racked his brain for a reason to refuse. The VC turned to him and smiled understandingly—a letter from on high, after all, quite natural to be a little awed—and then said, 'Of course you must be a relation of...'

'No, no, I'm not,' Prabhakar hastened to reply, wondering if that could be the reason for the letter? Whatever the reason he could see no way out. He would have to go and get it over with. He told the messenger he would be there.

Four o'clock tomorrow would come when it did, it was seven o'clock this evening that concerned him, drinks at his apartment to which she had said she would try and come. He was sure she meant what she said and was not putting him off in a polite way. It could be the nature of her work that made her uncertain and if so, the thought of it drove him to an anxiety close to desperation. The art of loving demanded that the loved one be shielded from all danger, a rule to be religiously adhered to, but it was one he was helpless to do anything about.

Prabhakar got into his car, drove out past the tank and turned right, heading for the shopping mall that had everything. The friends he had invited would be coming in any case even if she didn't, so drink and snacks had to be bought and ordinarily nuts and Haldiram's crunchies would have been enough for a usual casual get-together, but if she came… He knew nothing about her likes and dislikes. He only knew what he had read about her at her trial and the brutally frank and hair-raising account she had given of all that had happened. He had never expected to meet her. And then he had met her, last week, at Francois's place. And his future had become unthinkable, inconceivable without her. The time came to say goodbye all round, walk to the door and out into the corridor where his hand on the door should have clicked it shut behind him. But he had gone in again like a man possessed to ask her if by any chance she might perhaps be free on Wednesday evening, around seven o'clock, and just in case, had jotted down his address on the paper napkin beside her. He had hardly expected her to say yes to a stranger, was overcome by her maybe, and this was how she might be coming, or not coming, this evening at seven.

He made his way to the cheeses. At Francois's he remembered seeing her break off a bit of biscuit, push it into a ripe soft cheese and scoop up the melted part in the middle. Its name was unknown to him. He described what he needed to the salesman behind the counter who asked, 'Do you want Swiss or French?' Prabhakar had no idea but at Francois's it might have been French. He walked past the Parma ham, lingered at rows of high-priced foreign tins and bottles and picked up Spanish olives, an Italian artichoke paste and a jar of anchovy-garlic spread. From the wine section, a French wine he recognized. He went back to the Parma ham. Watched it being sliced razor-fine and layered on waxed paper which was then neatly folded and packed for him to take home. He was not spending sensibly and was well aware that sense had little to do with the state of being known as enchanted.

In the car his phone pinged. A high whining voice thanked him sing-songly for 'shopping with us and we hope you will visit our cheese counter again and our'—he switched it off.

'What's this, a celebration?' exclaimed Rahman. Salma, his wife, surveyed the spread and said, 'Of course, silly, the new book!' She traced an exaggerated adab to Prabhakar before throwing her loving arms around him.

There was no way to explain it was not about the book. The others were coming in. The room was filling with affection and exuberance and suddenly with celebration. At its high point Lopez tapped a glass for attention and raised his own to hail the book by 'the brainiest, luckiest, and goddammit it's not fair, he's even the best-looking bastard of us all!' Prabhakar responded to the high spirits around him with equal abandon, agreeing with Lopez. Privately his gratitude for fortune's favours knew no bounds. He had friends he could not imagine being without, work of his choice and a satisfying life. It was too much to expect another favour yet every nerve in his body ached for the doorbell to ring. Glances at his watch told him what he already knew, that time was passing. At half past eight he gave up hope. Hours later he woke abruptly and lay awake endowing the tank and the sing-song litany on the phone with sinister possibilities. He had not known that fear was the other side of love. His last waking thought was of her, held safe in his sheltering arms.

~

The house was in a crescent of private houses. Prabhakar was warmly greeted.

'I thought we should hear about the changes in Europe. It's a time of critical changes, as it is here,' said the eminence, 'so I've asked a few people who can enlighten us. Not officials or government representatives. They have to be careful what they say. These are men of influence whose opinions matter and are not afraid to speak out. There's a film-maker and an art dealer, a jeweller and others as you will see.'

The doors of the spacious room opened outward to the verandah. A light rain sprinkled the garden and washed the dust off grass and trees. 'Here we can relax and talk informally,' he continued, 'From our side your contribution will be especially valuable. Your book has got to the heart of the question of change when you say that lasting societal change will need an altogether new mindset.'

The Master Mind's name was Mirajkar and it was well known he was an eccentric who preferred to do things his own way, more or less invisibly, influence being most effective when least seen. He was fifty and elegant, a political theorist reputed in his field and advisor to the regime in his spare time. Two of his invitees were standing on the verandah, others were arriving. Prabhakar heard French spoken, and German, and some other language.

They settled down. Sofas and armchairs had been drawn into a roomy circle for conversation. Cups of tea, pastries and sandwiches were served in a pleasant tea-time atmosphere. They were different nationalities, together here because never had Europe been so much of one mind. So said the Austrian, a publisher of children's books, who obligingly spoke first only because someone had to start. This frame of mind, he clarified—and he was certain the others would agree—was concerned about the threat to European civilization.

'As we are about the threat to ours,' put in Mirajkar like an amen, and asked him if they were taking measures to deal with the danger.

Prabhakar was acquainted with the changing mood in Europe and had acquainted his students with the return of the crooked swastika, the stiff-arm salutes, the goose-stepping and its other street corner manifestations, but he had never met the Mood. Here it was, uniting Europeans as they had never been united. This is how it is and what is being done about it, he heard them say. There is a passion now evident all over Europe for an end to intrusions, nay invasions by outsiders. We must seal our borders to keep outsiders out. Keep Europe secure, keep Europe pure, keep Europe Christian, in a word, keep Europe European rolled like a refrain around the room. Prabhakar sat back in his chair, baffled and bemused. Europe had conquered the world. Europe had intruded, invaded, occupied, ruled and plundered the world. Could power and fury, power and glory, feel so besieged? There was no accounting for history's twists and turns but here was a twist of psychology. He was completely out of his depth in that realm.

He listened to the action being taken by the Mood: graffiti and flyers and leaflets to warn the public of present danger, parades carrying the swastika to keep their presence in the public eye, and public meetings to rally the like-minded. The mood is ripe. There is a response. Results will not be long coming. Meanwhile enemies of the state within the state have to be identified and dealt with along with their friends and sympathizers. Mirajkar interposed to say there could be no unity and no harmony without the removal of those who conspire against it. The Swede, or was he a German, wryly suggested putting muscular men in charge of that operation as had been done so successfully in the 1930s. There was no denying that muscled men left an indelible impression on people's minds.

And on their bodies, thought Prabhakar. But judging by what he was hearing, all this street fervour was still in the street. It had not yet entered bedrooms and kitchens. The time had not yet come for today's Europeans to talk in whispers, keep their curtains drawn and their doors locked. The time had not come to go into hiding or try in desperation to escape, as their parents had had to do. He hoped it never would. He stared at the man who was starting to speak. His head was shaved up the sides and back of his scalp, leaving a half inch of bristly hair upright on top. In his halting English he was saying the Slovenska Pospolitost, the Togetherness Movement in Slovakia, had results to show. Fourteen of their members had been elected to Parliament. In Slovakia the hour of fascist revival is already here.

'Two hundred of we Slovaks went in procession to lay flowers at the grave of our wartime leader, Jozef Tiso, in Bratislava, him who the Allies hanged as a war criminal in 1947. This was the murder of our national hero. But now it is we who decide who is criminal, who is hero. Now we remind our people of the better times we had under him. At his statue we made a vow to him. We said—as you can see it is written below this picture what we said—"You are ours and we will forever be yours."'

He passed around a photograph of the event. He and the other leaders of the procession were dressed alike in black suits, white shirts and red ties, and they all had the hairstyle. The silence in the room was impressive.

It was not possible for Prabhakar to get up and leave. Mirajkar was asking him to tell our European friends about his book, which they had not had an opportunity to read but they would be gifted copies of it. He pointed to the copies lying gift-wrapped in silver paper and red-ribboned on a table outside the circle. Prabhakar sat up. Telling them about the book was what, he supposed, he had been invited here to do. His book, he said, had been a flight of imagination, not changes he was advocating. It was an intellectual fling of his own invention. It was the kind of fling he indulged in when he wanted, well, a holiday from the classroom and from the rigours of academic discipline. It had come about because he had wondered what it would take to bring a complete about-turn in a society's ways of thinking—using his own society as an example, of course—and had reasoned that it would have to take the direct opposite of the ideas and images society had been taught to respect and revere: hallowed images like the Buddha deep in meditation, the Edicts of Ashoka preaching peace and righteousness, and in our own time the familiar figure of Gandhi, which was inseparable in people's minds from non-violence. These would have to be done away with, wiped out, dug out and destroyed wherever they were found, in books, paintings, sculptures and road names, on roadsides, in museums, wherever, so that they would be cast out of individual and collective memory. The virtues they now represent—renunciation, repentance, compassion—would be forgotten. These very words would disappear from vocabulary and any remaining rags of that inheritance would be despised as effeminate and degenerate. To excavate a society out of its age-old moorings and remake it, ruthless measures would have to be taken.

'Do go on,' Mirajkar urged, noting interest and absorption around the circle of listeners.

Prabhakar went on to say it could be done. In a manner of speaking Sparta had done it in BC by abolishing childhood. Six- and seven-year-olds had been removed from home to barracks to be schooled in war till they were eighteen. It was a martial upbringing teaching them that defeat in war would not be tolerated. Come back with your shield or on it, they were taught. So in a way it was an end to the time long associated with mother love and mother care. The children were kept barefoot and barebodied in punishing conditions to harden them to pain and privation. The result? Spartans had become the fiercest fighting force of their day. A little ripple of applause came from the circle. Mirajkar waited, then said gravely that the example of Sparta was a fascinating historical example. He was sure they would all agree it was now a time for bold initiatives, for strong men to take the lead, and forceful new images to replace tired old ones. Prabhakar's book had shown the way. Prabhakar interrupted to correct that impression but the party was over and the Europeans were saying their goodbyes.

Mirajkar was at the door seeing them off. He detained Prabhakar to ask if he was related to the

Prabhakar who was their late great founder and fountainhead of their thinking.

'No, I'm no relation.'

'Is that so? I was sure I was not mistaken. The originality and boldness of your argument—you don't mince words and you are not afraid to shock—all this being so similar points to a familial way of thought. I was even sure I saw a facial resemblance.' He smiled, 'Oh well, at any rate you are, as I myself am, from the same native earth as our revered founder.'

As Prabhakar was taking his leave, Mirajkar said, 'I don't know why a man of your intellectual calibre shouldn't be one of our policy group.'

Prabhakar excused himself. His teaching and writing took all his time.

'I understand. And we need our best minds in the universities to purge them of Communist and other atheist teachings.'

Of his childhood, Prabhakar had few actual memories. The rest of his background he had put together through his reading and research. It was factual reliable information that gave him a fairly good idea of the background he was seeking, but it was the bits he himself remembered that were the living link, the beyond-doubt connection with his lost past. He clearly remembered brick dust. It rose and fell in thick gritty gusts from the back-breaking brickload being hauled onto his father's bent-over back and carried far off by him to be unloaded on a mountain of bricks piled high for use. Brick dust drifted, veering windward from the mile-high top of the building under construction. It drifted down into hair, eyes, fingernails and toenails on the ground. It got coughed up, sneezed out, spat out.

He remembered squinting up the dizzying height where his father's naked toes gripped the bamboo scaffolding. Far below he and his barefoot playmates played catch-me, learning to dodge rusty nails and screws, iron filings and other wounding rubble. There was an open ditch they shat into, a tap in the open for drinking, washing and bathing when water came and before it suddenly went. He remembered the tin sheeting of the shed he and his family lived in. It roared and rattled when rain beat on it and when the sun scorched the sky it burned like fire. They had left that tin shed behind for this tin shed on this new construction site. Prabhakar read that poverty drove workers, the ones classed as unskilled, from their homes and made migrants of them in search of mazdoori for a living wage. Mostly they were hired where hard labour was in demand over and under the ground, in sewers and on roads, highways and building sites where they cleared and cleaned the ground, dug ditches, mixed concrete, hauled loads, erected scaffolding, picked their way skyward, and plastered and painted what they had built. If these were not skills, what were they? What was the meaning of the word? thought Prabhakar. These were skills that had to be learned untaught and untrained. They were learned the hard way, on the job. There was no regulated count of the bricks piled on your back or consideration of the weight your back could carry without breaking. No course taught what load you could jog with without losing your balance, or how to climb up a scaffolding toehold by toehold. No teacher warned: This is how, or you will fall to your death.

A study he read said there were no canteens, no toilets, and no drinking water on sites, no shoes, no helmets, no safety precautions. No crèches for babies, no care for the young who roamed where they liked unattended. The list of 'noes' went on and on: no contract, so there was nothing in writing. No eight-hour day. Work hours were elastic, uncounted and stretchable to as long as eleven per day. Workers were paid or underpaid or late paid, and unpaid for overtime. There were laws but the commonest law seemed to be the builder's bounty: fortified cane or bamboo underfoot, or only as sturdy as it came from the tree; platforms to stand on at towering heights, or none. It all depended. It sounded as if what the study called the bulk of the workforce lived or died as luck would have it. What must it have been like to work in such conditions? What inbuilt fortitude made it possible?

The nomads his parents had been remained anonymous and untraceable. He had only known them as Ma and Pitu and his grandmother as

Nannu. That was all he knew about the three who were his family and all he would ever know, there being nothing in writing to trace them by. Nomads have no address. Illiterates leave no trail.

There were other remembered scraps: the stranger who came and joined their catch-me. He pulled funny faces, wiggled his ears and twitched his nose, making them roll about laughing. He swung them around by their arms and took them piggy-back riding, galloping them turn by turn round and round the site and up the road and back, and galloping away with one of them. They never saw their playmate, or the stranger, again.

He must have been four or five years old when the windstorm started whirling brick dust in circles, thrashing treetops and whirling one treetop off its tree at the edge of the site. The wind gathered fury. The bamboo bent and his father's foot lost its grip. He saw his father's leg swing out helpless, frantic for a foothold, his flailing arm finding no handhold, his body hurtling down to hit the ground headfirst. An avalanche of loosened bricks thundered down on his mother who squatted below, her hand shielding the rotis she had brought for him. The wind swallowed his own wild wails. The storm brought his grandmother out of the tin shed.

On some day after that Nannu took him to the 'bhaktin ischool' which was not a school but a refuge run by the bhaktins of the Kolkata Mother who had set up rescue homes like this in other cities and whose bhaktins picked up the diseased and dying from gutters to let them die in dignity on beds. Nannu didn't leave him on the doorstep, trusting he might be taken in as some newborns and other unwanteds had been according to those who knew. She sat herself down on the steps to wait—for how long he never knew—and sat him on the step below her, locked between her spindly legs. Dry-eyed but distraught and hoarse from loud mourning she made the situation as audible as she could in words, and with ample gestures when words failed, to the bhaktin who opened the door, informing her she was committing the boy huddled at her feet to the bhaktin's care: this child of her daughter who was killed by brick thunder when her husband's death-fall split his skull open at her feet. Nannu bent and put a finger on his mouth and then on her own to make it doubly clear that the child was mute. He had not spoken since the bamboo bent and the bricks thundered down, not eaten, not slept. The bhaktin, who till then must have assumed the crumpled motionless heap on the doorstep must be ill from natural causes, made a sign like a cross over herself.

What had become of his grandmother after that and where she went Prabhakar would never know. He devoutly hoped she had made her way back to the home before migration and wished she could have heard him speak again as shock dimmed and utmost horror receded into some crevice of consciousness where it got stored like broken furniture in an attic. He attributed the return of his voice to the statue in the chapel, a figure of grace and sweet, surpassing gentleness, though he knew none of these words at the time, only the feelings her figure stirred in him. She wore a long blue robe. Her head was covered. Her eyes were cast down. Her arms hung by her sides with her palms turned a little outward. He had been told she interceded with higher authority for those who needed help because she had borne unbearable sorrow, and seen and suffered indescribable pain. Her presence reached out and enfolded him. One day he spoke. At night he slept.

He learned to read and write and read and read. He ate hungrily and as avidly devoured all that school could teach him, in the Catholic school run by their church that the bhaktins later sent him to. The day came when his schoolmaster in senior school told him he had been admitted to college and would need a surname. Prabhu didn't know where he came from, which would indicate the name with the name-ending he should have, so the master tried hard to think of a name, any name that would go with Prabhu. He came up with one that sounded something like it, hoping it might be easier for the boy to remember. Memorize it, he instructed, don't forget it. It's your name. And Prabhu Prabhakar he had been ever since. Prabhakar was how he thought of himself and the person he had become, though he was Prabhu to his friends.

They ordered their favourite brain masala at the dhaba that had expanded and now called itself a café, written 'kaif' in Hindi, and known as kaif to its customers. It had added a low rung of office workers to its working class clientele and a plastic menu of 'continental' choices. The time-honoured age-old irreplaceables were down at the bottom of the menu. Fortunately progress had not affected the brain masala, or the gular kebabs they could get nowhere else, or the rumali rotis that Rafeeq, the cook, made at their request. Prabhakar and Rahman went there for lunch when they wanted to catch up. It was far enough from the university to avoid meeting the VC's busybodies and their favourite as far as food was concerned.

'What was it all about? How did it go?' Rahman asked and Prabhakar described the tea party.

'For some reason Europeans feel they're under siege, and the Master Mind thinks we're under siege here. I kept wondering if I was hearing right. Why was I invited?'

'You wrote a book,' said Rahman.

He signalled a server for more of everything.

'You must be the last innocent left if you think a book is just a book. As it happens, and as you are always prompt to point out, you're not the first person to have written this kind of book.'

'What kind?' Prabhakar's bewilderment was complete.

'A terrifying story like no other. Mary Shelley wrote one two hundred years ago,' said Rahman.

Prabhakar had not heard of it. He waited for more.

'She wrote a novel in which a science professor called Frankenstein creates a grotesque uncontrollable monster out of chemicals and human remains. That's what you've done, Prabhu. You've written a story in which good and evil change places. You've created a monstrous scenario.'

Prabhakar brushed that aside impatiently. 'But it's a fantasy, Rahman, it's an exercise of my imagination. You know that. I was spinning a yarn.'

'So was Mary Shelley. Only her yarn stayed on paper. Yours might not.'

'Good God, that would be a nightmare.'

'It would.'

They paid their bill and went out behind the kaif to the kitchen to pay their customary homage to Rafeeq, and give him a small token of their appreciation for their feast. Rafeeq threw up his floury hands in resignation, indicating his shrunken domain, now that it was shared with the 'continental' cook.

The following day it became official. Bharat was no longer Mata. From now on Bharat was Pitrubhumi. Fatherland. And from now on females above the age of seventeen would be addressed as Devi as a mark of respect in a culture which revered women.

Francois and Prahlad had a wide and varied acquaintance. It was at Francois's that Prabhakar had met Lisette. Named after, she was telling someone, her grandmother's favourite Maurice Chevalier song. She sang a line of it: 'Eyes of Lisette, the smile of Mignonette, the sweetness of Suzette, in you array...'

She was attractive in her unaffected spontaneity. 'What's the rest of the song?' Prabhakar asked.

'Grace of Delphine, the charm of Josephine…' She laughed. 'Oh, I can't remember the rest of it but it ends with "You are my ideal, my love parade." *Love Parade* was the name of the movie it was in.'

She was called away and disappeared from view. Her foreignness and air of sophistication kept him from seeking her out again. But after a while a pleasant surprise. She was back with a drink in her hand and sat down in a chair next to his to talk to him. About a business matter, it turned out. She was in India to look into the food scene, not for Michelin—there were other respected connoisseurs who gave star status to restaurants—and she was going to be touring around investigating on behalf of one of them. But could he suggest any outstanding place here before she went south? Francois and Prahlad's Bonjour with its accent on peace and quiet at breakfast, its delicious offerings and its lovely Indo-French ambience had been a discovery. And what darling people they both were. Yes, her assignment would include the people who owned and ran the places. It made for an all-round picture. Could he suggest any places?

Prabhakar had never heard of Michelin (or for that matter of Maurice Chevalier) and wanted to say he didn't eat out much, it was too expensive, so he was the wrong person to ask. Then, suddenly annoyed with himself for holding back on the diet of emperors—what a betrayal—he said he did know a place.

'Oh, wonderful! I'll write down the name and address.'

'It doesn't have an address. It would be hard for you to find, it's off a road in an alley. If you like I could take you there.'

'Would you? If it's not too much trouble? I'm intrigued.'

He regretted his offer immediately it was impossible to picture her in the kaif—but now it was made. On the appointed day, a day of sullen heat, he drove her through the bazaar traffic of cars, strolling cows, buffalos and three-wheelers, off the main road and down the alley to the kaif. It was lunchtime and crowded. Fast fans whirled the stagnant air high above them. They found an empty table under a fan in the middle of the lunchtime clamour. A server swung his jharan off his shoulder, wiped spilled water and some sticky stuff, flicked a blob of chutney off the table and swung the jharan back on. Lisette mopped her forehead with her handkerchief and looked around.

'This is more like it,' she said, 'Something a bit different.'

Prabhakar had forgotten the true researcher's obsession with research. He ordered lavishly and with care.

'I'm familiar with Indian food,' she assured him while they waited, 'Curry is very popular at home.'

'Curry? Which Indian food are you familiar with?'

'What d'you mean, which?' Light dawned. 'I see. Of course. How absurd of me. It's as if I'd lumped smorgasbord with ravioli.'

'Exactly,' approved Prabhakar. 'We'll be eating Mughal.'

Later, ignoring the trickle of sweat streaking down her cheek, she was concentrating on what she was eating, 'Great gourmets those Mughals must have been. It's impossible to guess what spices have gone into this, it's such an amazing blend of so many flavours.' A little later, halfway through the meal, she was astonished by the taste and texture of the kebab she had bitten into. 'I've never eaten a kebab like this, it's pure silk, and who would have thought of putting shredded orange of all things into a kebab! I would never have believed it.'

'This particular kebab was invented for a toothless old Nawab so it had to be soft as silk. The royal khansamas were experimenters. They had to be, to produce new delights to please royal palates.'

'Or get their heads cut off?'

'No, nothing of the sort, they were far too valuable. And they probably ate the same food, plenty of leftovers. As far as that's concerned Islam has no big divide between master and servant.'

'I can't thank you enough for bringing me here,' said Lisette after her heartfelt appreciation—hand on heart—had been translated to Rafeeq in the kitchen, and he, squatted among a clutter of utensils, had responded as graciously, hand to brow.

She was still under the spell of Rafeeq's cooking on the way to her hotel. 'And to think he does all this in that tiny space, in that heat, with no machines to mince and grind and blend, only that helper. The man is a magician. And what about all those recipes? They're obviously in his head. But where d'you think they originated? Along the crossroads between Europe and Asia? In Persia and Arabia and Arabian Nights places to land up here and become Indian?'

Prabhakar had not thought of gular kebab and rogan josh in those romantic terms, taking it for granted that most things Indian were mixtures of here and elsewhere. He said it was the same with music, dance, language and a hundred other things. But Lisette was intent on what she had eaten and a write-up that would be her most original, featuring Rafeeq, and not the kaif's owner, as the person who mattered in the kaif.

'You've been so kind,' she said, 'I'd never have known about this place but for you. Can't I give you a cup of tea at my hotel?'

She agreed to have it at his place instead, where

she pottered around his bookshelves while he made it, spotted his book about fashion, sat down with it, and asked if she could borrow it. She would take it to read on her food travels over the next couple of weeks, she said, but would come over before she left for London to say goodbye and return his book.

'There's no need to return it, Lisette, please keep it.'

Over tea, 'You've never married, Prabhu?' she asked, not inquisitively. She was enquiring in her usual keenly interested fashion.

'No. Marriage among us needs antecedents. Background, family, uncles and aunts, all that paraphernalia. My parents died when I was a child and I have no relations.'

'None? Not one?' She considered that, absorbing—or so it seemed to him—the consequences of that lifelong deprivation.

She came anyway to say goodbye, saying she knew him much better after reading his book and had enjoyed Josephine's amorous goings-on. What a fun way to look at history and such fun to read, like Ten Sixty-Six.

Prabhakar told her it had been fun to write.

It wasn't very sporting of Bonaparte to desert Josephine, she said, considering his own Polish affair with Marie Walenska, not to mention his child by her.

'But I'm sure you know, Prabhu, that was why he had to tear himself away from Josephine. She couldn't have a baby, and as he was going royal, he had to have a legitimate son.'

'Yes, I do know. That's a fact of history. But all that muslin must have given him a good excuse, don't you think?'

'I'm sure it did!' she laughed.

She had brought her write-up about the kaif for him to read. It described accurately what she had eaten, with some history and geography thrown in: food that had journeyed, linking far-apart cultures, transporting robust feasts of flesh and fowl along with delicate creations of spun sugar and syrups, wafting flavours and aromas across borders to become native to wherever they were eaten, and for Mughal to become forever Indian. This conclusion marked her in Prabhakar's eyes as someone distinct and discerning, as down-to-earth as she was romantic, and never confusing the two. He had not expected her to remember his remarks about assimilation or to take them seriously.

There followed a description of Rafeeq's work space cluttered with gas cylinders and brass cookware, its odours of garlic and cloves, its mountain of potato, onion and ginger peel, and the splutter of hot oil where mutton sizzled in a redolence of spices. From this cubbyhole of a kitchen had come the magical meal she had eaten. Her last sentence caught Prabhakar unprepared. It crowned Rafeeq with 'a skill that defied working conditions'. For Prabhakar it was the highest accolade that could be bestowed on one of the millions who laboured unheard and unseen.

Time and distance had put him beyond the reach of unmanageable sorrow. What had taken its place was a silent seething anger against those who turned a blind eye to skill. They must be the grossest among humankind who did not know skill when they saw it and made use of it, and for whom human life was expendable and cheaply replaceable. He got up and gave the pages back to Lisette and thanked her fervently for her understanding. She could not have known what he was thanking her for or what was going through his mind but she seemed to understand its emotional importance. She hugged him impulsively and said they must keep in touch.

A week after the Wednesday which was the day she had not shown up, Prabhakar found time to look for the bunch of newspaper clippings of the trial a few months ago that he had put away among his files. No trial could take place for want of evidence, they had said. The dead could not be questioned and no survivor had come forward, no eyewitness, nobody. Told-to accounts after the event could not be taken as evidence. But the noise about it would not go away. And then she had come forward.

She refused a lawyer—who could afford a lawyer? She and her colleagues certainly couldn't. She said she would speak for herself. She asked the judge the regime had chosen to head the enquiry commission they had set up, to guide her in procedure as she was ignorant of it and did not want to disrespect it in any way. Asked what organization she belonged to, she said none. None? Then with what authority and under whose auspices had she come forward?

'On our own. We're a voluntary group, Your Honour, myself and four other women from different countries who've seen what massacres did to women in Serbia, Bosnia and Rwanda. We came together to find out what was happening here and we divided the affected areas among ourselves.'

So hers was an eyewitness account? Yes, she had been there at the time. She had been in the village she had been allotted, where most of the families were Muslim.

The clipping said the judge could barely conceal his impatience. If she had been there at the time, why had she not come forward then? Her brief reply was hardly heard and he must have decided not to pursue that point because she had gone on without pause or preamble to say: It was still daylight when the mob came...

Came where? Be specific, from the judge. Name

of village given, she went back to the beginning: It was still daylight when the mob came yelling—yelling their war cry... and threw lighted branches around to set the village on fire. Families rushed out of their homes and ran in every direction into the fields. The mob ran after them. And after us: me and three of the village women and their children. The wheat had been cut and we kept stumbling on the stubble until the woman who was very pregnant could go no further. They caught us and beat our legs with iron rods and forced us to the ground.

The clipping said she spoke in an expressionless monotone. The thought of it gripped Prabhakar, as it had the first time he had read the account. It conjured a cultivated deadness and eyes glazed with unsheddable tears. Had she dulled her voice to mesmerize herself into a somnolent state so that she could speak the unspeakable? She was told to speak up. Her voice rose: I said they beat our legs with rods and forced us to the ground...

The judge ordered silence or he would have the court cleared. He would have ordered a separate room for her testimony but she refused and said it must be heard, and continued: They pulled our clothes off. More men came. They dragged us apart to make room and kicked our legs apart. Each of us was surrounded and held down…

Prabhakar could not go on. The sentence hit him harder than it had when he first read it. Now that he had met her, he saw her surrounded and forced down. He knew he must reread the rest of it but it would have to be later. His immediate need was to meet her and offer her his support in whatever way. There had been no chance to talk to her at Francois's and now it was an anguished necessity. Too much time, a whole week, had been lost. He rang Francois for her telephone number and Francois said wait a minute and gave him the address as well. He dialled the number, heard it go on ringing, six, eight, more times. The next thing he knew he was on his way.

The house was in a quiet corner of a shady lane and if there had once been a name on the gate, it was no longer there. The high wall on either side of the gate was embedded with jagged broken glass. The short path to the house was hedge-lined and unevenly pebbled—it would be rough on shoe soles and hard on tyres—to discourage visitors? He bumped his car up the drive. The front verandah was curtained off by low-hanging bougainvillea. A house in purdah.

He was admitted to a room whose furniture was minimalist and geometrical, all straight lines and sharp corners. Not intended for lounging. Flamboyance lined one wall in a painting of war-like shapes in a blaze of discordant colours by a famous painter of a massacre during the exodus of the Partition. The polished floor had scattered rugs that he could not help describing to himself as woven of bleeding red and bitter orange. A stark room that said, state your business and go. He had not planned what to say and he had no idea how he would explain his presence. He remained standing.

A door behind him opened and closed. He turned around to see she had come in. She was all in white, white cotton sari and a white sleeveless choli that forced his attention to a raw-looking ugly patchwork of ridged scars along her naked upper arm. The repellent sight made him go swiftly to her and hardly realizing it, put his arms around her.

His shock was immense when she gave a strangled scream of a cry and broke violently free of him. Striving for composure, she sat down, motioned him to a chair and covered her face with her hands.

When she raised her head she said matter-of-factly, 'It was the contact. I can't manage physical contact, any kind, any more.'

The enormity of what she had said, and left unsaid, kept him from saying anything at all. It was the difference, the great void between reading about it and seeing it for oneself. He grappled with her problem. There were times that called for the crutch of religion. He didn't know if that crutch was available to her. He had none to offer—he had no religion other than reason—but the scripture of his childhood had been Christian and it had been awash with miracles. The miracle of the loaves and fishes, water miraculously made wine and most miraculous of all the command to a corpse to get up and walk, which the corpse obeyed. Lazarus stood up and walked as if he had never been dead. Nothing less than a miracle of that drastic order would restore her fully to the world of the living.

Her 'Will you have a cup of coffee?' eased the high tension.

She remembered meeting him at Francois's. She had not been able to let him know she couldn't come last Wednesday because he had not given her his phone number. The coffee was hot, strong and reviving, a painkiller of a kind. The atmosphere scaled down to nearly normal. She had spoken frankly and unsparingly about herself, and this allowed him to be as plainspoken, telling her he knew about her ordeal because he had read the evidence she had given at the trial. Would she look upon him as a friend, could they meet and talk, could he take her out occasionally, getting out and about would surely help. A puzzled look greeted his proposal. This was what she was doing, getting out and about. That's how they had happened to meet. In fact, meeting people and being sociable had been prescribed as therapy and the psychiatrist had called it a necessary part of her treatment after her abortion and her stay in hospital for other damages. She had been doing as prescribed, as well as getting on with writing her report. But, yes, it would be nice to meet. The report? She and her colleagues were writing their accounts of the areas they had been assigned as well as their own earlier personal experiences and these were going to be published as a book. By a feminist press abroad as the new law about womanly modesty would ban its publication here.

He asked, hardly daring to, but horribly aware of her butchered arm, if her injuries had healed as far as possible. The outer ones had healed, yes, but as he could see they had left their permanent reminder. It was policy—decided by herself and two of her colleagues who had been raped in other such wars—to leave their outer wounds exposed. Rape had been hidden and talk about it forbidden for too long. And besides, she, who for some reason fate had let live, had a duty to her tortured and slaughtered companions and their little children, and must let her wounds speak for them.

She offered him more coffee. Frank and forthcoming though she had been—a matter of policy as she called it—she had kept off any mention of her invisible wounds and the interior havoc of rape that made a human touch unendurable. He knew that trespass into that zone would not be permitted. He understood as if she had said it that the frigid wasteland she now inhabited was one she must find her way out of alone. But yes, she had acknowledged that life did have to go on.

At home that night he knew he must finish reading her testimony before he met her again, this time with greater attention, to understand what she had been through and what he was up against if he was going to be of any real help to her. He spread the press clippings on his dining table, weighted them down and continued from where he had left off:

They pulled our clothes off. The youngest of us, she was a beautiful young girl, fought them, shouting and struggling against being stripped naked so they cut off her breasts to silence her. The pregnant woman was on one side of me. They kept hitting her swollen belly, beating it to abort the foetus before they got onto her one by one. The waiting men laughed and egged them on, showing their own penises and kept yelling, 'Now we will make little Hindus inside you.' One of them picked up the woman's son, threw him face down and forced himself into the boy, telling the child, 'Without castor oil in your arse we will make you holler.' You see, Your Honour, she said in the same expressionless monotone, looking up from the paper from which she had been reading, their voices were much louder than our cries—they wanted to make sure we heard them—that is why I have been able to read you their exact words. Above us we heard them say 'Use them as much as you can, don't let a single one go.' Not even the three-month-old baby that one man picked up and smashed on the stubble. The woman on my other side begged for mercy for her two little girls but they took the two terrified little children and raped them in front of their mother, and then her in front of them…

All this while there was no silencing order from the judge. None needed. The exact words had produced a rapt silence. She put down her paper.

'About me, Your Honour,' she continued in the same monotone, 'Two men dragged my arms up. A third one grabbed my breasts and clawed and scratched them with his nails while the fourth man was raping me. Then more men came, eight more. And raped me one by one. Nine of them altogether. On the other women I cannot say how many, I could hear nothing, see nothing any more… When they were done with me one of them found a rod they had beaten our legs with and hit me with it, on my stomach and my body all over. I was dead to pain by then and I must have lost consciousness because they took me for dead, after making sure with the rod that I was… By then they must have been in a hurry to go. When I came to, it was growing dark and they had gone. I tried to move, I tried to get on all fours to crawl, to look for my companions, but I couldn't move. I could only turn my head to one side and I saw thick black smoke coming from a fire the men had lit some way off. It told me that was where my companions were, thrown in to hasten the process because they were taking too long to die… I don't know how long I lay there till two of my colleagues came looking for me… took me away…'

The judge's grave conclusion: A most unfortunate event, most condemnable. And that it should happen to one in your position… The work of unknown miscreants. Best forgotten.

Prabhakar assembled the clippings in a neat pile and laid them back in their file. He got up and put the file back in its place in the steel chest of drawers he had taken it from. It was imperative to stay cool and rational. Life after rape was his problem now, not hers alone. And there was no such thing as a modern miracle.

No miracles, he reflected, yet there had been inexplicable events. Not quite the same thing, but he had come across a compelling one a year ago when he was preparing a lecture he was to deliver on Gandhi. It had happened to an American journalist. Prabhakar took Vincent Sheean's book from his Gandhi bookshelf to refresh his memory. He had found the book absorbing. Foreign correspondents were a breed whose forte was facts, not unexplained and unexplainable events. Sheean himself was known for his wide coverage of the brute facts of the twentieth century: the rise of fascism in Europe in the 1930s, the Spanish Civil War and the Second World War. He had met and reported on every wartime leader across Europe and Asia. And then he met Gandhi.

Prabhakar opened Sheean's book to the part that led up to the unexplained event. He had come to India and met Gandhi, had long talks with him and travelled with him to understand the workings of a political mind whose war without violence had made world news. Bizarre the command he had given his weaponless army of followers: If blood must be shed in this battle, let it be your own. Unheard of his political philosophy that had nothing to do with politics but began and ended with what had to be done for those whom he called the last and the least. Sheean had never met such a personality in politics, and he had met everyone of consequence. The meaning of his encounter with Gandhi became stupefyingly clear in his powerful description of what he went through on the evening of the 30th of January 1948:

He was in the garden of Birla House at five o'clock on 'one of those shining Delhi evenings' along with other foreign correspondents and the people of Delhi streaming into the garden for the daily prayer meeting. 'I felt well and happy and grateful to be here,' wrote Sheean. About ten feet away, Gandhi, with a shawl covering his bare chest against the chill, was making his way slowly through the garden, across the lawn from where Sheean and other newspaper men were standing, to go up the four or five steps that led to the prayer ground. Then came 'four small, dull, dark explosions.'

'What followed must be told as it happened,' wrote Sheean, '(to ME, ME) or there is no truth in it.' Prabhakar read Sheean's account of what followed those explosions decades ago. It was still painful to read and still profoundly moving: 'Inside my own head there occurred a wave-like disturbance which I can only compare to a storm at sea—wind and wave surging tremendously back and forth ...' Sheean had leaned forward from the brick wall he was standing against, doubled up and 'bent almost in two.'

'I felt the consciousness of the Mahatma leave me then—I know of no other way of expressing this: he left me. The storm inside my head continued ...'

At the same time he became aware of a burning

stinging sensation in the fingers of his right hand, and tears unlike tears, that were more like acid burning his eyes. When he was able to look at his fingers he saw blisters on the third and fourth fingers of his right hand. They were filled with water. There had been no blisters before he heard the shots.

What flooded into Sheean's mind as he described this discovery was the 'many many' dreams he had had night after night the summer before in Vermont, dreams of trying frantically, and failing utterly, to thrust his body, his arm, his leg, any part of himself between Gandhi and his inevitable murder. He kept reliving his desperate dream-efforts to shield Gandhi and be killed in his place so that Gandhi would live. For days after the assassination in Delhi he was obsessed by the horror and agony of his failure 'to die for the Mahatma, the last best hope of earth.'

The blisters—would they be stigmata? Prabhakar looked up stigmata. His dictionary called it 'marks resembling wounds on crucified body of Christ'. Sheean made no such exalted claim. Days later, when he could at last function normally, he concluded that the blisters, which had appeared the instant the shots were fired, were 'a psychosomatic phenomenon', by no means new to science. Psychosomatic, Prabhakar confirmed, meant 'resulting from interaction of mind and body, or influence of one on the other.' Sheean had accepted this scientific explanation but it had not replaced his conviction that the blisters were proof of his connection with the murder he had forseen in his dreams and his calamitous failure to prevent it, in reality as in his dreams.

Explain them how you will, there are still and always will be wonders that will amaze us. It was an idea Prabhakar would have liked to discuss with her. In love there is a longing to share. What did the beloved think of Sheean's remarkable experience? What would she think of the Iranian film he had seen a week ago or the spy thriller he was reading? How had she reacted to the election in Nepal? Much as he longed to make love to her, he longed as much to know her in all the ways that make for discoveries between two people. She herself had said life had to go on.

He had learned about sex the way one does, gaining knowledge and experience as one goes along. Love had not needed learning. He had known it since birth. In a remembered scrap of memory he lay between the two who loved each other. He grew from birth to infant to child lying in the small narrow space between their bodies every night. When they thought he had fallen asleep he would be shifted aside with tender care, letting them reach for the comfort of each other after the hard, heavy day spent apart. Their sighs and murmurs assured him they had found each other, and he could fall asleep knowing they were where they belonged, inseparably joined. At some moment of remembrance long after he had lost them he had come to believe that if it had to happen, it was more merciful this way, for neither of his parents could have lived without the other.

Prabhakar tried to decide what kind of film he could take her to that would interest and entertain her, take her mind off what had happened if only for an hour or two. At this point he was not even sure they would ever meet again though she had seemed willing. But this came about not long afterwards.

Prabhakar and Rahman were going to the kaif for lunch and took Lopez who had never been. In high anticipation of the meal they had promised him, they ordered. The server looked helpless. The owner was sent for, arrived, jammed his palms together, and stood there in harassed pleading posture before two valued customers and a third esteemed guest. He apologized in a lowered voice. Rafeeq away, no Mughal. It was irritating, but it was too late to go somewhere else so they settled dejectedly for hamburgers. The plastic menu informed them these would be chicken in the bun, no longer mutton, the real thing.

Lopez reminded his friends: no meat unless proven to be mutton, not cow. The Cow Comission went around making sure. He was thinking of becoming a vegetarian himself, he was scared as hell that his fridge might be raided and the mutton turned into beef. Suspects were being dealt with out on the streets, surrounded by cameras and cheering beholders. He didn't fancy that treatment for himself.

It was far from reassuring in view of Rafeeq's disappearance or dismissal. They drank their cloying Limcas, not sure how to find out about Rafeeq. The kaif's water wasn't safe and there was no mineral water left. All the bottles of mineral water had been commandeered by 'them', the 'they' and 'them' who came and went, mysteriously unnamed.

Lopez, who taught Modern Europe, said, 'This tea party you were at, Prabhu, you said the Slovak was well ahead of the others.'

'Why wouldn't he be? They've had practice. They had a flourishing Nazi republic during the war, with a Gestapo and Jew-disposal and all the trimmings, and evidently there's a tremendous nostalgia for those good old days when everybody was kept in line, or in harmony, as they called it. Togetherness was the watchword. Not that the other speakers weren't harking back to the glories of the 1930s, but I did get the feeling that some of them were sitting back and waiting to see which way the wind would blow before they risked investing in it. Only fools rush in. Compared with the rest of them the Slovak was the only Boy Scout.'

'But most people are little people who have to go along with whatever's happening,' said Lopez, 'either because they don't know any better, or they have no choice and can't afford to lose their wages or their lives.'

'Most people,' repeated Prabhakar, and again with stubborn emphasis, 'most people everywhere, in Europe or here or anywhere else, only ask to be left in peace to live their lives. It doesn't seem too much to ask.'

Rahman broke in on their reflections on the rise and rise of fascism. 'Look here, Prabhu, we must go and see Rafeeq as soon as possible. He'll be in need of work and help, poor man.'

He lifted a hand to signal to the owner, who came. No, the owner did not know where Rafeeq lived. The server who arrived to remove their plates of half-eaten chickenburgers did know and told them, after darting a look right and left.

Prahlad had told Sergei he was going to dance for a special occasion and Sergei thought it was typical of him to return to his art for the occasion. It would be his way of celebrating what must be the first or the second anniversary of Bonjour. The party was to be at Francois's apartment which was larger than his own. Their other friends were already there when Sergei arrived, sitting on cushions on the carpet in a room that had been cleared of furniture. A hypnotic tabla beat sounded from the shining floor beyond the carpet, against the sliding sound of strings being tuned. A sofa had been left at the back of the room for those who were unused to the floor and Sergei who had come in late sat down there. He was feeling like a drink but no drinks were on offer, which confirmed his impression that Prahlad did not believe in disturbing or diluting effects. This, he guessed with some amusement, must be a personality trait, and had nothing to do with any highbrow conception of art. Prahlad had even taken care not to disturb Sergei's breakfast, letting him eat his Eggs Benedict in peace before coming to talk to him.

Sergei listened to the leisurely tuning of the two instruments to the perfection required. He found it curious, this display of making ready in front of an assembled audience, instead of appearing with tuned instruments ready to perform. Could it be that involving the audience in the tuning up was a traditional part of the performance, a way of involving the audience from beginning to end, like saying: We are one, united, not separated, by Art. Be with us, not way out there. There was a suggestion of that in the seating arrangement that had artists and audience at the same level, all on the floor. It was far removed from a concert in the West which is sacrosanct unto itself, brilliantly illuminated onstage and cut off by pitch darkness below and beyond. He allowed himself to relax. It was pleasant to be thinking about matters other than work. There was no niggling worry about what might be needing his urgent attention. For many years he had flown in, and mission accomplished, flown out of countries. He had seen the sights in some but he had not felt what a much-travelled acquaintance of his called the pulse, or heard the heartbeat, of any. Now that Ivan had taken over in New York—grandson of Dimitri with the business acumen Dimitri would have been proud of—and his own capable deputy was in charge in London while he was away, he could look forward to more time to himself. Starting now.

The tuning was done, the rhythm begun, and Prahlad was dancing. He had a partner, a young woman from the troupe he had belonged to. Her embroidered bell-shaped skirt swayed from side to side, twinkling as light glanced off the tiny mirrors sewn all over it. She wore a satiny top and a headdress like a little cone with a transparent veil drifting over it. Prahlad's costume was as graceful, a dhoti that left his legs bare to the knee, and a green satin or velvet waistcoat. Their movements were small, subtle and sinuous. This was not the dramatic demanding dance called kathak which Sergei had seen performed in Edinburgh, with its controlled facial expressions and gestures, its breathtaking spinning and subsiding, and the mathematical exactitude of its rhythmic footwork. Watching kathak he had been reminded, for lack of any other comparison, of Chopin's minute waltz. It was the timebound discipline of both. He mentioned this to the woman who had come in after him and sat beside him on the sofa. A comparison she would never have thought of but yes, she agreed, it was an interesting point. And of course the dance we are watching is entirely different from kathak, though this, too, is a classical dance. We have so many classical dance forms in different parts of the country, all very different from each other. This one is from the northeast, it's called Manipuri and it acts out the love story of Krishna and Radha. That's why Prahlad chose it. It's dainty and delicate, as you can see, but it has its own discipline. The beauty is in the wrist movements. Watch the fingerwork and the way the dancing feet lift off as if they've flown up. Sergei watched as directed and saw she was right. He decided Manipuri must have been created for long thin fingers like Prahlad's and bodies as light and nimble as those of the two performing artists.

It would seem so, she agreed, but she wanted Sergei to know that this performance was not pure Manipuri. Prahlad was improvising. Since he was not with his troupe any more he hadn't been able to get the drummers who would have been drumming and dancing around him and his partner, or to borrow the cymbals and the rest of the classic accompaniment.

'Being Prahlad, I think he just wanted to dance, no matter how, for this important occasion. For him there isn't any better way to celebrate. I think he must have been born dancing.'

Her voice had the warmth and affection of a caress and it made Sergei turn to smile at her. His glance jerked away. He was unable to suppress a shudder at the sight of livid reddish skin showing above her low-cut blouse. Not a skin disease. It was something incomparably worse. It looked inflicted.

She said to his averted face, 'Manipuri is from our northeast and I'm no expert but they say it has influences from the countries around us, even from as remote as Siberia. Isn't it incredible how cultures travel and blend?'

No one applauded when the dance ended. Something else seemed to be starting. The musicians took their instruments away and a silver tray was brought in, of miniature clay oil lamps—called diyas, she explained—and set down on the floor. Prahlad and Francois, dressed like Prahlad who was still in his silk and velvet Manipuri costume, came in and sat down crosslegged in front of the tray. Behind them a voice was chanting.

'The diyas are in place of the fire there should have been,' Sergei heard his neighbour say softly, 'and the mantras being chanted are the ones actually recited in the service.'

Sergei was mystified but could ask no questions—he had not got over the shock of her ravaged skin—as Prahlad and Francois got up and started stepping around the tray of diyas. They walked around it several times in single file and then out through the door into the drawing room. The floor sitters, already up, streamed after them. There was an outburst of rejoicing. Congratulations were called out amid loud laughter and the popping of champagne corks. Francois and Prahlad, bedecked with jasmine garlands someone had brought, were at the centre of it all. A cry of delight from Prahlad when he saw Sergei. He took his arm out of Francois's and made his way to him.

'You remembered, Sergei! You are a friend of the heart!'

'How could I forget, after all the breakfasts I'm enjoying at Bonjour. Is it the first or the second anniversary of Bonjour?'

Prahlad fell back, mortified. 'I didn't tell you? It is our wedding day. We have just got married!'

Francois came to them. Glasses of champagne followed.

'We couldn't have a civil marriage or get a priest to marry us,' he said, 'because our marriage is illegal, Sergei, we have broken the law. So Prahlad decided to do things his own way. He loves ceremony,' spoken like an indulgent lover.

'I'm so glad I could be here,' said Sergei sincerely. 'Let me wish you both lifelong happiness.'

They drew him into a three-cornered embrace, called for more champagne to toast each other and drank. Prahlad put his glass down, lifted his arms high and clapped his hands. Faces turned towards him. 'These are tragic times,' he announced. 'The times are grim, and so, my friends—let's dance!' This was greeted with enthusiasm and when

Francois, choosing from his Italian collection, put 'Signorina Cappucina' on the player, everyone danced, in pairs without touching or athletically on their own, unlike the intimacy of the ballroom dancing Sergei had known, with your partner held agreeably close. Those who knew the words were singing. The winsome young woman who had partnered Prahlad came to Sergei, her bell-skirt swaying, and said 'Dance?'

'I'm sorry, I wish I could but I can't,' he apologized, but she urged 'Come!' and took him firmly by the wrist. At the edge of the dancers she lifted her arms, twirled and untwirled her fingers and went into variations of Manipuri to the rhythm of 'Cappucina', leaving Sergei to devise variations of his own, which he found himself doing.

Prabhakar suddenly saw her, exquisite as ever. She was talking to Prahlad on the other side of the room. It was a gift he had least expected, and thanking whatever gods there be, he wound his way through the dancers to spend the rest of the evening with her.

The wedding buffet, laid among tall lighted candles and fresh flowers, created a hush. Francois put love and longing on the player to accompany it and beckoned his guests to the buffet as a voluptuous voice began singing his and Prahlad's favourite 'Al-di-la' in Italian and then its English version 'Beyond'.

'Beyond the most beautiful things, beyond the stars, there you are, just for me... Every star will light the way above me to where you are... Just to measure your worth I'd move heaven and earth to be near you... You're my life, you're my love, you're my Al-di-la ...'

The song drew Francois and Prahlad irresistibly together in an emotional moment no one disturbed.

'Al-di-la' had its trance-like effect on the diners, which was why it had taken Sergei some time to get back to the question in his mind: What had Prahlad meant by grim and tragic times? Sergei had joined his sofa acquaintance—who he now knew was the dear friend Prahlad had wanted him to meet—and another guest at a table in a small alcove off the dining room, and was taken by surprise when she said, in Russian, that she would try to answer his question. Her mother was Russian and had named her Katerina, 'So please call me Katya as my friends do.' It accounted for the rare arresting beauty of her father's dark skin displaying her mother's green eyes and Slavic cheekbones.

There is no doubt that each language makes an impact all its own. Sergei found the impact of what she was saying more searing in his mother tongue and hers than it would have been in English. Prabhakar who knew the facts well, listened to her calm recital with deep misgiving. Could it be right to repeat and rerepeat this monstrous tale? Should pain be probed and prodded over and over again? As she went on he began reluctantly to see why she thought it necessary. If those who survive don't tell the tale, she had said, it will be forgotten. The agonies of those women and children, their pain, their horror and terror, not just mine, will never have happened unless we tell it. Telling it passes it on, makes it our heritage. It's because tales have been told and retold that we have a *Ramayana* and a *Mahabharata*. Our epic horrors are no less our heritage.

When she had completed her personal story she said Sergei should be given the larger picture, not just her bit of it, and asked Prabhakar if he would go on with the rest of it.

The haunting declaration of love that was 'Al-di-la' would have been ruled out as unsuitable background music for barbaric acts onscreen in cinema, but Prabhakar could not separate 'You're my life, you're my love' from the barbaric assaults on her body and his intense desire to rid her of that memory.

'Prabhu? Could you tell Sergei … ?'

'I'm sorry, yes of course. I was wondering where to begin. I might as well start with today. I was driving to the university this morning—I go past the Gandhi statue on Mall Road …'

A statue unlike the usual standing or sitting statues of heroes in public places, he told Sergei. It was unlike the military heroes majestic on horseback, with the horse's front leg upraised if the hero had been wounded in battle, and both front legs upraised if he had been killed on the battlefield. This statue neither stands nor sits. It walks, as pilgrims do. This is—or was, he corrected himself—a sculptor's rendition of Gandhi's most famous walk.

In 1930 he had walked from his ashram at Sabarmati to the seashore village of Dandi. He was sixty years old. It had taken him twenty-four days, stopping at villages along his way, to walk the two hundred and forty miles. He was walking to the coast to make salt from sea water in defiance of the British government's Salt Law that made Indian ownership of India's salt a criminal offence, and the Salt Tax an added burden on the poor.

Prabhakar had told his students the Salt March had been a unique event in politics. Gandhi had made no call for others to join him in breaking the Salt Law, but a trickle of followers had become thousands who joined the march at stages along the route. Across the country men and women made salt where they could. An Englishwoman walked with Gandhi. An Englishman wrote and people sang:

> With dear old Gandhi, we'll all march
> to Dandi,
> And break all the salt laws that a white man
> ever made.

Prabhakar had told his students this act of civil disobedience had become an ecstasy of civil disobedience. The power of civil disobedience had stirred people across nations and nationalities, and across the years. Thirty-five years after 1930, Martin Luther King and six hundred others had walked fifty-four miles from Selma to Montgomery in Alabama in their refusal to bow down to racial segregation. A month later two thousand more men and women, black and white, had marched again to Montgomery, walking all day and sleeping in the fields at night. There are ties stronger than blood, Prabhakar had told his class. There are ties beyond blood, beyond borders, beyond race and religion. Beyond.

'And this is why you stopped at the statue?' Sergei prompted.

'No, this is not why,' said Prabhakar.

He had stopped and parked across the road because of the demolition squad at work on it. They broke the legs first so that it would never walk again. This made the stone body fall forward for easy battering and breaking—as that other demolition squad Katerina had described, had done on women's bodies, disabling their legs first. He stayed to watch a machine pound the fallen body and lift the crushed stone to the storage space on top of the machine. He stayed watching the destruction to the end because it was a statue he would never see again. He stayed to say farewell to a unique political event and a page of Indian history—and as history has its human side, he stayed because Rahman's grandfather had been among the thousands who had walked with Gandhi on the Salt March.

Prabhakar felt a prickling like tears at the corners of his eyes and willed them not to fall.

'What about the procession of statues behind Gandhi?' asked Katerina, 'the people who followed him on the march? Did those statues get bulldozed too?'

'Those are still there, I suppose because they'll be following the statue they're planning to put up in Gandhi's place.'

'Anyone for Slivovitz?' Francois was beside them, gaily waving a bottle of plum brandy and calling for liqueur glasses. He poured it for them, said Salut, and Zdorovye to Sergei, and took the Slivovitz away.

'Something that happened a few days ago was much the same,' said Prabhakar, getting back to what had to be said, 'so demolition must be official policy now.'

He had gone with Rahman to the cemetery where Rahman's father and grandfather were buried, which his friend visited on their death anniversaries. On that immaculately kept kabristan, earth was being overturned by a giant excavator, digging up graves. Earth was flying and fragments falling in showers of bones and other human remains. An ancient tree had been felled and split open, obscenely exposing a century-old welter of ancient knotted roots. The guardian of the graveyard who had come from Moradabad as a young grave digger and grown old as its caretaker, sat at their feet, bowed over his knees, unable to watch this desecration of the last sacred resting place of the departed. The land was a jungle when I came, he wept, we made a garden of it for those who had left us. Sometimes we found bones while digging a new grave. Reverently, we would collect them, and place them prayerfully in the new grave we were digging.

To Rahman's question he had no answer or none he could bring himself to utter. The excavator's driver only knew he had orders but he told Rahman what he had heard: Burial is against our religion, we do not bury our dead, grounds that have been captured for burial will be dug up and prepared for national use. Rahman raised the old caretaker to his feet—they had on occasion stood side by side offering namaz in the mosque near the cemetery—and pressed the few hundred-rupee notes he was carrying into his hand. He'll be out of a job now, Rahman told Prabhakar, and homeless. He had been given quarters nearby for himself and his family and had lived there all these years.

Prabhakar clasped his friend's hand and stood holding it in shock and shared grief.

Sergei broke the solemn silence that followed Prabhakar's recital, saying, 'In Europe we think of wars about religion as belonging to the Middle Ages.'

'Here we are back to the Crusades,' said

Prabhakar, 'Our Popes have declared war on Islam.'

Sounds of happy leave-taking were coming from the hall. Thank-yous, long-drawn-out goodbyes, invisible hugs and kisses. Sergei thanked Prabhakar for giving him much to think about. Turning to Katerina he told her in Russian he had no words to express his sorrow for what she had been through.

'Not only me, Sergei. It's the treatment, and not just here. You must have read about the civil war in Yugoslavia in the 1990s, the one that eventually broke up the country.'

He must have, at the time, but it had made no special impression—one more Balkan disaster—and had soon become yesterday's news.

'Thousands of Muslim women—Bosnian, Croatian and Albanian—were rounded up and kept in camps to be raped by Christian Serbs. Those camps got known as rape camps. It's what war does to women but this was something new. Religious rape. Like here.'

It sounded fantastic in the extreme, a situation conjured up by a diseased and deranged imagination.

He had a passing doubt about the size and scale of it. So openly organized, would it not have made news outside its own terrain?

'One knows what war does, Katya,' he said slowly, 'Who doesn't? But I had never thought of it in terms of what happens to women.'

'No,' said Katerina, 'No one does.'

He acknowledged that yawning blank in the reckoning of war's damages. It reminded him of scorched earth laid waste and infertile by retreating armies.

After Sergei had gone, she bestirred herself and picked up her small silk purse. 'I must go. It's late.'

Prabhakar's mind had never been clearer than at this late hour of the night, and never so intent on making itself clear.

'Yes, it's time to go,' he agreed, 'but first there's something I want to say. You may be right that the tale has to be remembered and made known. Remember it and make it known if you must. But there's a life beyond that tale, a full and normal life.' He added, half-humorously, 'There's even a belief among us that there are lives beyond death.'

He looked hard at her, holding her gaze, 'So Katya, Katerina, however you wish to be called, there is life beyond gang rape. That's all I have to say except that I love you.'

Katerina pushed back her chair and stood up. 'Beyond must be your favourite word,' she said.

Unbelievably, she held out her hand. He took it with care, held it lightly, not imprisoning it with his other hand, and let it go. When the time came he would have to be as delicate with all the surfaces of her beautiful body in his awesome task of freeing her from her terror of being touched.

At his hotel Sergei phoned his daughter.

'Have you thought of a name, Daddy? Mum says you will want to keep names Russian in the family. '

'Your mother is right, Irina. We'll name the baby Katerina and she can be Katie for short. How is she doing?'

'Simply splendidly. Tom and I took her on an anti-war demonstration yesterday. That way it was easy for me to feed her when she was hungry and we could take turns carrying her in the sling. What? Oh, the sling is like a pouch you hang on your front.

It's a pouch to put the baby in. We put Katerina in it and she was snug and secure held against me—or Tom when he took over.'

'Irina, how old is she now?' Sergei tried to keep his agitation out of his voice. He knew better than to argue with Irina.

'She's nearly two months old.'

'And which war were you demonstrating against?'

'All war, of course. At last there's a politician who believes in unilateral disarmament like Tony Benn did. If he forms a party we're going to support him.'

Sergei tried, for his newborn granddaughter's sake, for fear of her being carried into the dust and uproar of future demonstrations slung in a sling, and for the sake of his own peace of mind to say cautiously, 'Well, there's no war on right now so there's no immediate need for action.'

Irina said wearily, as if she had said it time and again on public platforms—which she might well have done—yet with a consuming unfaltering passion, 'Do you realize, Daddy, that somewhere, in some part of the world, people are living in dread, scanning the sky for bombs? Somewhere else people are running for their lives in a city that's being devastated? We've heard Never Again so often, it's a joke. Daddy, there is nothing so certain as the certainty of the eternity of war. So someone has to say Stop.'

Sergei was well trained in her beliefs. Her single-mindedness always disturbed him afresh. What it was up against in a violent world was most disturbing of all. He tried to keep a recurring vision of physical harm to her out of his mind. Purity of heart was no protection against weapons of war. He was consoled by the thought that she and Tom had moved at his suggestion to the spacious upper floor of his apartment—once Susan's studio—after the baby's birth. To his relief they had agreed to give up their own two-room flat 'until we find something bigger we can afford. And it makes sense, Daddy, with all that space lying empty since Mum left and you away so much.'

He bid her a gentle goodnight and said he would be seeing her and Katerina very soon. He made no move to go to the bedroom and prepare for bed himself. The talk over dinner crowded out any notion of sleep. Finally, Dimitri's voice: No concern of ours. But Dimitri had not heard what he had heard tonight.

In the morning a late breakfast at Bonjour helped to restore his steady reliable perspective of affairs and he could look forward to the prospect of a morning's sightseeing. He ordered an unpronounceable, subtly flavoured Indian breakfast dish and ate it with new-found pleasure. The coffee surpassed itself. He glanced around the room. These particular paintings and tapestries which Francois and Prahlad had chosen with knowledge and care, and hung just this harmonious distance apart, in an atmosphere they had ensured would be unsullied by the vulgarity of competing loudness, had made for a space of order and beauty within four walls. Peace on earth in miniature. Wise men know this is what is meant by peace on earth and that we cannot change the world.

The telephone rang that night on his return from dinner with his company's agent.

'Sergei? It's me, Susan.'

He panicked. 'Is the baby all right? Irina?'

'I'm sorry I startled you, Sergei. Everyone's all right. I'm ringing to put your mind at rest. Irina told me you sounded worried when you talked to her.'

'I was frantic. I didn't know it showed.'

'Well, I'm ringing to say I've persuaded her to leave Katerina with me when she has to go to her meetings and demonstrations and she's agreed.'

His relief was profound. Only Susan could have persuaded her. Susan had always been a confident mother, well able to take care of their two children during his frequent absences and it was obvious she had lost none of her sure and sensitive touch, based on their mutual respect for one another's opinions. Their two children, but for Susan, might have gone their separate ideological ways without a care for each other, Sergei acknowledged in silent gratitude. He asked if she would come to dinner the day after he got back so that they could have a family evening together. Susan was doubtful. She was having dinner with Philip and his new author to show them the rather unusual cover she had designed for the novel Philip was publishing, but she would try and change the date. Since Sergei had first met her and wooed her, her politics had been confined to the book covers she designed. A cover she had designed for a biography of Hitler had shown him a tiny figure in the lower right-hand corner, with Wehrmacht marchers glitteringly occupying the main cover front and back.

Prabhakar pushed aside the papers he was correcting to answer the telephone. It was Lisette. She was buoyant. She had glorious news. She was getting married next month to the owner of the set-up for whom she had investigated Indian food and they were going to open a restaurant. It would be the only one of its kind in London or anywhere in England. It would be purely Mughal, with décor to match.

'We want Rafeeq to come here. With his family, of course, if he has one. We'll make all the arrangements as soon as he agrees. Could you talk to him and let me know?'

Normally Prabhakar would have asked her how this would be possible with the immigration hurdles now being put in place, and impossible at any time for people like Rafeeq, but the bare fact was 'He's not at the kaif any more.'

'Why ever not? Where is he?'

Prabhakar cast about for a way to explain that would not sound like gibberish, but there was no rational explanation. 'Rafeeq is not at the kaif because it's not safe to cook mutton any more in case the Cow Commission says it's beef.'

'You're joking, Prabhu,' she said, incredulous, 'And then what?'

'Then you're arrested, or worse. You could be killed.'

'What's happening?' she demanded, 'I don't understand.'

Prabhakar had seldom been at a loss for words but what words were there to describe what had never happened before. Never here. A new gross jargon would have to be learned. As Lisette was struck dumb he continued, 'So there's no Mughal cooking at the kaif any more. There's no Mughal anything any more, not even the empire. They've taken it out of history books.'

Lisette recovered to say vigorously, 'But that's

absolute nonsense. It's as daft as saying we never had the Tudors, all the Henrys and Elizabeth One. It sounds as ridiculous as a nursery rhyme I learned when I was six years old:

> Hey diddle diddle, the cat and the fiddle, the cow jumped over the moon,
> The little dog laughed to see such fun and the dish ran away with the spoon.'

'That explains our situation perfectly,' said Prabhakar.

'Well, I don't understand what it's all about,' she said, getting back to the purpose of her call, 'but we have to have Rafeeq for our new restaurant. He's authentic, a real find. No one else will do. Look Prabhu, I know he'll be nervous about coming here. It's a big step for him to take. But you must persuade him, and tell him he won't regret it. We'll take good care of him and if he has children we'll put them in school…'

'Lisette, Rafeeq is not at his home. There's no one there. If I can find him I'll let you know.' How he would find Rafeeq he had no idea, but the effort would have to be made. Lisette was a person who saw things through. 'And congratulations. Your news is wonderful.'

'I'm in heaven, Prabhu. But we must have Rafeeq.'

A suggestion came from Katerina at dinner that night at Rahman's. 'Rafeeq's home must be in one of the areas they're driving people out of and setting fire to, like the village I was assigned and other villages around there, or digging up grounds like the graveyard. They call it taking back the land occupied by invaders.'

Rahman had been unlike himself, unnaturally subdued since the excavation of the graveyard. It was Salma who asked where the villagers driven out of their homes had gone. Katerina didn't know, but one of her colleagues and co-writer on their book project had said that in her country the policy of wiping out a religion had herded whole families into camps, made displaced people of them while it was decided what to do next. These were very primitive makeshift shelters with no proper sanitation or water supply or electricity. People had to rig up their own electric wiring and scrounge around for wood to cook on.

'How did she know? Did she see one of these camps?' asked Salma.

'She lived in one of them. She was one of the herd driven into them. She said guards used to come at night and separate the women from the men…'

Katerina sensed violent recoil like a live presence in the room and gave it a minute before continuing, 'We will have to find out where those villagers are, if they've been put in a camp, and go there.' Another second of silence told her no one else's mind had jumped ahead to that course of action. 'Of course, Rafeeq may not be there but that's where he's most likely to be. We'll have to go and see.'

She must not go with them, they protested. Rahman, with his habitual tenderness for mankind and more especially for womankind, said it would be exhausting and emotionally too much of a strain after all she had been through. As if she hadn't heard, Katerina told them she would make enquiries tomorrow morning and go with them. She had never met Rafeeq and wouldn't recognize him, but Rahman had said he had a wife and two children so she would ask among the women. It could be useful. It had to be agreed she would go with them tomorrow afternoon after classes, giving her the morning to find out where the camp, if there was one, was located.

At the sprawl of tents, hutments and flimsier shelters concocted out of tin and tarpaulin, Katerina suggested they divide up for a thorough search for Rafeeq, not just look around for him but keep asking if anyone knew him or had seen him. Prabhakar took the direction given. He had not imagined quite this. There was a finality about this mass removal, clearly no hope of escape from it. There would be no going back to where they had come from, or forward to elsewhere, for those expelled from their village lands and their livelihoods who now had nothing to do and nowhere to go. This squalor had no shape or form and no connection with anything he thought of as human habitation. Yet human voices were telling him they knew no one called Rafeeq; the sun was beating down on barefoot children chasing each other through the mud of narrow alleys between shelters or playing marbles in the dirt; an infant howling behind a makeshift curtain of cloth thrown over a rope, was soothed, lulled, and must have slept; cooking fires were being fanned, hot sparks flying into the hot air. He walked on through the sound of men's voices, the chatter of quarrelling children, a woman pounding clothes in the scanty water from a tap—signs of humanity obstinately alive in the nowhere of displacement. In a patch of shade two old men squatted, staring into space. They, at least, had recognized the permanence of their plight. Coming to a tent at the end of his area he called out and lifted a tent flap by its corner, hoping to get some information from those within, and let it drop, paralysed by his transgression. A woman labouring strenuously to give birth lay on straw matting on the ground, her legs wide open, her body writhing, her groans unmindful of all but the merciless rhythm of labour. The woman keeping vigil between her legs had paid him no attention.

He walked back, his stomach convulsed by the sight and sounds of birthing, the ultimate act in defiance of extermination.

On their way home, an hour's drive, Rahman at the wheel, there was little to be said about the failure of their mission. Their separate silences bound them closer than talk. Prabhakar, sitting beside Rahman, felt sickened at the thought that Rafeeq might have been beaten to death and his body left rotting on some roadside. Where could his family be hiding and how long could they hide? He understood why Rahman had nothing to say. In deep mourning for the man he had known, for the faith they had shared, and for their brotherhood with all others under the Indian sun, what is there to say? Prabhakar turned to see if Katerina was all right, more out of his need to look at her, an opportunity that rarely came his way. Her head was leaning against the seat back, her eyes were closed, her mouth slightly open. Her hands had fallen far apart as if unrelated to each other. One must have slipped off her lap and lay looking lifeless beside her on the seat, the other looking as lifeless on the other far side of her lap. Sweat had left her hair limp and lank on her shoulders and dried on her face, leaving a damp sheen of it on her forehead. Sleep had released her to an abandonment that the discipline of her waking hours did not allow. He had never seen her more desirable or loved her more passionately than in this unconscious disarray. As they got back to town their jerky progress through traffic woke her and she directed Rahman to her house. There was a semblance of a return to ordinariness in her instructions to drive straight on, turn right at the next crossing, it's the last house in the lane. At the porch overhung by its curtain of bougainvillea, she said, 'Come in and wash and have a cold drink.' Automatically they obeyed. Cooled and freshened by soap and water, sipping their ice-filled glasses of lemon juice, they were somewhat revived but not yet recovered from what they had seen, and fearful of what might have happened to Rafeeq. They thanked Katerina for coming with them on their expedition and being of the greatest help.

Katerina shook her head, frowning. She dismissed their thanks. What were they talking about? Of course she had had to go to see the camp. It was vital to keep track of what was going on. Hadn't they realized there may be other camps, considering the new policy? Her voluntary group might decide to do an investigation into these. She added as a matter of interest, 'One thinks one's own is the ultimate catastrophe, and of course it is, but only for oneself.'

'An investigation?' echoed Rahman in disbelief, 'Like your last one? Would that be wise?'

Katerina was astonished that he should ask such a question. 'No,' she replied, 'Of course it wouldn't,' and saw them out to Rahman's car.

American voices filled the room that was full of Indians. Trays were offering American cocktails among other drinks.

'I've heard so much about you, we all have. What a pleasure to meet you. Mr Mirajkar has told us about your book and your presentation at his get-together.'

The woman's voice had no cocktail party bubble about it. The woman herself, in solid middle age, looked like a person in authority. Prabhakar could see her chairing a meeting with professional ease, with an American insistence on the facts, figures and data which established proof. Americans were known to deal in ground realities, not fairy tales. They had Hollywood for those.

He had made up his mind to refuse this invitation to a reception for visiting dignitaries at the Century Hotel. Obviously, Mirajkar had put him on the guest list and he wanted to end his uncomfortable association with the Master Mind, but Rahman had advised, 'Better go. Get the atmospherics. As Katerina said, it's just as well to know what's going on.'

'Let me introduce myself,' she said, giving her name and the name of the company she worked for, 'I'm one of the VHA. We're the Voice of Hindu Americans—which makes us your voice in the United States—and I'm happy to say we're getting a lot of support from the administration. I know how worried people here are about the new immigration policy—though in all fairness one can hardly blame the USA for clamping down on immigration, everyone is doing it—but my Senator is working on trying to get Hindus into the white category so our people here won't have to go through all the usual hoops when they apply for visas, or for citizenship.'

White category? She clarified this meant that though Hindus would not be in the privileged category of the European Union whose members needed no visas, they would be upgraded for entry to the USA, or for citizenship. 'If my Senator gets his proposal through it would make Hindu Indians honorary whites ... but I'm keeping you from helping yourself to a drink, here comes a bearer.'

The only drinks left on the passing tray were dry martinis and he took one. Recklessly. There was always a first time. He took a swallow of it and hated its harshness.

He knew he was being annoyingly slow to appreciate and applaud the VHA's role in this forthcoming achievement. 'But how can Indians be put into the white category?' he asked.

'Not all Indians,' she corrected, 'we've too much

of a muddle of races, which, of course, is being put right now, but no, no, this will only apply to Hindus, not those who came as invaders and other outsiders. We are the only ones who have a right to the white category. You know, Mr Prabhakar, there's an enormous amount of sympathy for what Hindus are going through here. But in any case there is such a thing as a racial hierarchy and we belong at the top, to the Indo-European racial category. It's been the VHA's job to acquaint the administration in the United States with this fact and we circulate it in the media and women's clubs and other influential groups. We're covering a lot of ground and we've had a generally favourable response. After all, it takes no great leap of imagination to understand a historical fact, and it's as much an anthropological fact. A well-known historian has vouched for it, as you may have read.'

Alerted by the martini Prabhakar noticed a map behind the cocktail bar at his end of the room. The cartographer had fancied an India extending from the Indus in the far north to the Arabian Sea at its southern tip as one unbroken landscape of lustrous gold. No obstruction had been permitted to mar the peninsula between the snows and the sea, no Afghanistan, no Pakistan, no Bangladesh. For the country he had invented, the cartographer-turned-artist had invented a colour, this pale lustrous gold never seen before on any map of any country. Prabhakar's informant followed his glance and nodded as if in complete approval of his dumb amazement.

'Makes one catch one's breath, doesn't it? Let's just say it's an artistic vision of the future.'

She greeted someone across the room and took her smiling leave. Prabhakar described the map to Rahman afterwards, saying it was not a figment of his imagination, and nor was the martini responsible for what he saw.

'It seemed to sum up the occasion,' he said.

'It sums up everything,' retorted Rahman.

The Sunday paper always had a lavishly illustrated supplement. Pictures of classical singers and dancers, film-makers, writers and other creative achievers—the truly great—as well as food and fashion, were splashed over its pages. But the American ambassador was featured under a headline on the front page of the main newspaper. Prabhakar read: 'The Ambassador of the United States, His Excellency Mr Jake Judson and his wife, are seen at the foot of the aircraft. In his farewell message Mr Judson said he had high hopes of India. It had been a privilege to serve here at a time when major changes are taking place and more are expected. He complimented the government for the reforms it had undertaken, and affirmed the alliance between "our two great democracies."'

There were times when Prabhakar, who was not a Communist, wished he was. This was one of them. He hoped Communism had a future. He turned the page. Nothing much there of interest. He glanced down the page and an item in small print caught his eye. Vandals had broken into a restaurant called Bonjour. The damage was yet to be assessed…

Prabhakar got no reply from either Prahlad's or Francois's numbers. He dressed hurriedly and drove to Bonjour. The cluster of flowerpots at the entrance to the stairway had been smashed, the hydrangeas and other blooms flattened under a heavy muddy tread. He went upstairs. The glass door to the restaurant was open minus its glass. He walked through its empty wooden frame. Prahlad was standing in a sea of shattered glass, facing a bare wall. The French paintings of springtime flowers that had hung on the wall lay knifed to shreds around his feet. The Tree of Life opposite had been pulled off its wall, scissored and trampled. Chairs had been overturned. Some lay broken. A table had lost its legs. Prahlad was in a state of shock. Prabhakar went up to him, took his arm and turned him around to lead him to an unbroken chair. Two men came in. One of them pushed Prabhakar aside. Prabhakar resisted instinctively, enraged. The intruder's arm swung out and hit him in the face. Prabhakar staggered backwards and fell. Blood smeared his face. He tasted it in his mouth. On his feet again rage drove him to retaliate. He was wrenched back by the other intruder who followed instructions to 'deal with him so that we can get on with our business.'

Prabhakar was dealt with. He was left on the floor gagged and bound with rope. 'Prahlad, is it?' he heard their wheedling voices, 'then why no divine protection if you are Prahlad?' Prabhakar heard and smelled a match being struck, blearily saw it held to the soles of Prahlad's feet and heard Prahlad's long-drawn-out howl of unbearable pain. And then once more. 'So, Prahlad you cannot be. Fire did not burn Prahlad. What are you?' One of the wheedlers enquired of the other, 'Do his kind at least have balls the same as us?' They pulled his pants down and dealt with what they saw. 'They're no use to the likes of him.' Prabhakar heard screams faded out by their laughter and then, 'Enough. The order was to smash the place and fix the dancer. No more holy dances for the likes of him.' He heard their heavy tread thudding down the stairs. A lifetime later he felt a movement ungagging him. Francois's voice said he had been at the police station, held up there like an offender and questioned for an hour. Prabhakar's rope was untied. He was helped to his knees and eventually to his feet. Rocking on his feet he helped Francois to untruss Prahlad. Between them they got his trousers on. He could not be stood up on his tortured feet. He had to be lifted down the stairs with help from Bonjour's cook who had stayed hidden in the kitchen. The day wore on as Prabhakar got himself down the stairs.

At the hospital Francois stayed with Prahlad. Prabhakar was examined by an elderly doctor who said it must have been a terrible accident. Thrown out, you say? Hit by a speeding truck? There were all too many such accidents these days.

Lies have to be told when the truth is too dangerous.

The abdominal injuries are severe and will take time to heal. An ice pack for your eye and your face. These medicines and it goes without saying a few days' rest in bed. But all things considered…The doctor, a kindly man with an old-fashioned regard for a patient's fears smiled reassuringly, conveying good, if not the best, news.

Prabhakar rang Rahman who came after his class and helped him into his car.

'What did the doctor say?' asked Rahman, 'No, don't talk if it hurts. I saw Francois. Couldn't see

Prahlad. He's in a bad way. How could this have happened?' he wondered, 'The Master Mind? His policymakers, considering their anti-nature, anti-religion, anti-our-culture tirades against gays?'

'And the Mood,' mumbled Prabhakar, 'Europe. Here. Everywhere. Hate. Kill.'

'Your fault, dost, you wrote a book, remember? Like Mary Shelley you let loose a monster.' A feeble attempt at a joke, but one that brought an effort at a crooked smile to his friend's swollen face. Rahman put an arm around him in a half-embrace.

At Prabhakar's apartment he helped him into bed, said he and Salma would come round in the evening, and left.

Bed rest allowed him the leisure to go over it all, but not the luxury of forgetting. The body had a memory of its own. On his third day of rest, the bell rang though he had requested friends not to come. This one called, 'Where are you?' and putting the ice pack aside he directed Katerina to his bedroom. She stood beside his bed. Looking down and right through his body on the bed, she said she had been to see Prahlad. Parts of him were better but he would never dance again. And you? Of habit he took in the startling beauty of her, unbelievably physically present in his room. He was all right, he said, just resting as ordered. Lies that had to be told.

'So I see,' she said, 'I've been away, I just got back so I just heard about it from Francois. I was in Leningrad with my mother, visiting my grandmother.'

There was something odd about that sentence of hers. What was it? Yes, Leningrad. It had not been called Leningrad for years. She should have called it Petrograd or St Petersburg, he'd forgotten what name it went by. Was she looking forward to a Communist future? His political mind told him that when there is one extreme, as there is here, you have to swing all the way to the other extreme before coming back to an ideal space in the middle. The feminists had understood that. During his lack of response Katerina had not sat down on the chair near his bed. Any moment she would be gone and he would be left with the times he had made love to her in his imagination, with a delicate care for her recoil from touch. Instead, a modern miracle. She lay down beside him and eased one arm around and under him. He felt it under his shoulder blades, supporting his back. Her free hand rested on his abdomen before tracing the path lovemaking took in a reversal of their roles, bringing his body, the corpse it had been, to ardent life. The holy books were not wrong.

Susan had been able to change her date with her publisher and came to dinner the day after Sergei returned. She had also rung Ivan and told him he must fly over for a day or two and meet his new niece—now asleep in her carrycot on the living room floor—and spend a little time with all of them. Dinner, ordered by Susan, had been a comfortable return to familiar home-cooked food after exotic menus abroad. Sergei had the weekend ahead for a long slow unwinding. He sat back listening to Tom and Ivan arguing. It was the kind of academic argument they had on the subject from time to time, by now without raising their voices, to reaffirm their known positions. As always it was well informed on both sides, with neither side (in Sergei's opinion) getting the better of the other, the subject being what it was and both of them being right.

Tonight Tom was asking Ivan what new weapon of destruction was on the anvil. In Tom's opinion, bombs and missiles and all that cumbersome heavyweight war-making stuff would be as out of date as bows and arrows very soon with all the new research into deadly chemicals that would make napalm look as harmless as lavender water. No armies and no armaments would be needed. Poisoning the air or making a drought would do the needful. Wouldn't that put the family firm out of business? Ivan said it would make no difference at all. He didn't believe weapons of any kind would be going out of date. Dimitri's grandson speaking, observed Sergei, with a loyalty to the family firm and a business-like commitment to its product that would have rejoiced Dimitri. He would have known the firm was safe in Ivan's capable hands. Sergei had never been able to summon the wholeheartedness that would have rewarded his father's efforts to build a future from scratch. All that Sergei had done in return was to put away his ifs and buts and follow his father, as a filial duty, into the business, working hard and commendably but with a secret sense of betrayal of the life he would otherwise have made for himself. Even then it had not been a matter of conscience but of the classics he would have preferred to indulge in, and an urge to write.

'The weapons you use,' he heard Ivan explain, 'depend on what kind of war you're planning to make—sky, ground, or chemical, or all three. And that decision depends on what you are aiming to destroy and what you have to be careful not to: the sites of copper or diamonds or oil or uranium or whatever your war is going to be about.'

From Tom: 'It also seems to depend on which country you're planning to attack and what colour the people are who live there. The atom bomb wasn't invented for Europe and all the baby atom bombs they've been dropping since then have been on Africa.'

'Well, there you have it, Tom. End of argument.'

Irina said, 'It's not the end of what's going on.

Did you know that in Nigeria Africans are fighting foreign oil companies for control of their own oil? What right do companies have to grab someone else's oil or uranium or other resources?'

'It's not about rights, Irina. It's about trade and being in control of it. It's what empires were about. Trade is what makes the world go round. You have to keep the upper hand. You don't need to occupy Asia and Africa to do that any more. You just stay in control by making sure your kind of people are in power over there.'

Irina countered, 'And knowing your guns could be bumping off an elected leader like Lumumba and so many others, you can still ... ?' Irina gave up mid-sentence.

Sergei drank his coffee, recalling that in his youth after-dinner conversation had been about books and plays, or the latest political scandal. Tom and Ivan would go on arguing, but there was no final answer—given the permanence of war—to the rights or wrongs of catering for it, which was the job of the armaments trade and a simple matter of demand and supply. The argument, as Sergei well knew, had no end. It had gone around in his own head since he entered the business his father had so painstakingly built. The two opposite views held by his children had kept it simmering, and the dinner talk at Francois's had given it a new lease of life. The sight of a war victim—which Katerina was—had made sure that for him the argument would not obligingly go away. Her wounds were glaring evidence of war and there was written evidence otherwise of the event she had unemotionally laid before him. But he had had a flicker of doubt about the camps she had spoken of, set up when civil war was tearing Yugoslavia apart. Large numbers obscure reality. Pain, one's own or another's, is hard to quantify, and memory can make mistakes. But he had looked up the period to establish the facts and found that Katerina had not exaggerated. The rape camps had been as real as the gas chambers. Women, as she had pointed out, had always been war booty, to be carted away with other loot by the winner. But this, she had said, was not that time-worn routine, it was different, and Sergei's information had left him in no doubt that the concentration camps for mass rape had been officially ordered, efficiently organized, and had served their purpose, it seemed, with spectacular success. Hard evidence had been provided by the international tribunal appointed by the court at The Hague to investigate the facts. It was obvious the camps were carrying out political policy of the gas chamber variety, as monstrous as that final solution had been, to isolate, despoil, and demolish large numbers of the unwanted. The court at The Hague had branded it a war crime.

There is no accounting for the particular moment that says enough is enough and there is no drama about the decision then taken. The responsibility for running an industry that depended on wars and catered for them had come to an end for Sergei when he verified the facts. He felt curiously light, unburdened and uninvolved as he listened to Ivan talk of supply and demand being the nature of the arms trade, and heard Tom replying that this could be said of a brothel. The argument ended in a draw, the young people discussed plans for the weekend and dispersed to their rooms. Sergei took Susan to the apartment he had bought for her, saw her safely in—old habits die hard—and said let's meet soon. He came home to think about what he would do in retirement, but one step at a time. His first step would be the book waiting these many years to be written.

He sketched out a rough approach at his desk over the weekend. Conquest, occupation, and control of the seized land's treasures were a long-established progression. Nothing new there. But never had seizure of lands and treasure been envisaged as a birthright until Cecil Rhodes. And never had politics, industry, and armaments worked in such harmony to achieve the desired result. In truth, there had been a symphonic harmony about the entire process with Rhodes as its conceiver, composer and conductor. What his country owed him had made a national hero of him. There were statues of him and a film celebrating 'Rhodes of Africa'. Hero-worship had inspired the 1892 cartoon in *Punch* of Rhodes, legs spread wide, straddling the length of Africa from Cairo to the Cape, his arms flung east and west, his body slung with an assault rifle that showed how possession had been accomplished.

The cartoon paid homage to a nineteenth-century Caesar, a colossus whose promise of 'Tomorrow the world' predated Hitler by decades. Rhodes' belief in his right to own Africa—'those parts that are at present inhabited by the most despicable specimens of human beings'—had come from his belief in imperial destiny, a phrase he himself might have concocted, and maybe he had, so smoothly did it serve his philosophy. Over port and cigars with policymakers and the moneymen of industry and armaments, he had laid down the doctrine of divine right. The white race being the master race, so ably represented by the English upper class, the British empire had a divine right to conquer and rule the 'uncivilized world'. He had shown how this could be done by doing it, combining in himself all three ingredients for control: He had become prime minister of Cape Colony and made himself de facto ruler of vast lands in southern Africa; he had spent extravagantly on armaments to clear those tribal lands of their inhabitants, for gold and diamond mining—'I prefer land to niggers'—and he had become a diamond billionaire.

All this was old hackneyed imperial sin, mused Sergei, leafing through his Rhodes material. The sentiments, the language, the 'destiny' that sanitized brutality were familiar features of long-gone imperial times and imperial crimes. What reading Rhodes made clear, however, was that a version of divine right still ruled the planet and the formula for the capture and control of commerce still relied heavily, if not always openly, on arms. A rose by any other name, or devil in disguise, depending on your angle of vision. 'Devil in Disguise' sounded like an apt summary of a post-Rhodes post-imperial world still bolstered by the force of arms and might be an apt title for a book. It was a curious situation in this day and age, but that being the case, was he, Sergei, to infer that by merely doing his job, as he had done, or by obeying orders as Nuremburg's accused Nazis had done, one missed the fact of one's own involvement in crime? By this logic had he been accessory to the murder of unknown millions?

It was after midnight when this vaguely disquieting night-time thought struck him. It was the sort of abstraction he had no use for, too vague, too theatrical. But daylight altered it hardly at all in his favour when by chance he came across a document he had not seen since his return, left among his papers by Irina probably, as she sometimes did to bring words worth remembering to his notice. This time it was a speech against the Cold War and all war. He read it with growing surprise. These were not, as he would have expected, the routine sentiments of a pacifist or anarchist or some woolly-headed idealist spouting the usual spiel. These were the words of a five-star general of the American army who had become president of the United States, in a formal speech delivered at the White House. Sergei read President Eisenhower's grim warning against the 'military–industrial complex', branding it a formidable threat to democracy, and, as his words suggested, to a just and humane society: 'Every gun that is made, every warship launched, every rocket fired, signifies, in the final sense, a theft from those who hunger and are not fed, those who are cold and are not clothed. This world in arms is not spending money alone. It is spending the sweat of its labourers, the genius of its scientists, the hopes of its children ... Under the cloud of threatening war, it is humanity hanging from a cross of iron.'

During the days that followed, Sergei's approach to the book he was going to write took a direction of its own, one he had certainly not intended. His own rough idea had been to narrate the fascinating story of trade in readable language for the general reader: from its quaint and colourful beginnings to international importance. But now that would be the first half of the story. The second half would go from baubles and beads to bombs; from footsore plodding to soaring threatening power; from Dimitri's escape for survival and the second life that made a fortune on arms supplied to specific wars. There was no shortage of material, preserved in the company's archives, of the figures made on armaments deals during the Cold War– he recalled Dimitri's example of the Communist bloodbath in Indonesia—and finally, the peacetime deals that had funded peacetime wars in his own time. What would this be, a much delayed reckoning? A confession to assuage guilt for crimes committed? A bid for absolution, as in the confessional? Sergei did not have a melodramatic turn of mind. He had no idea how the story would develop as he wrote it, only that in the light of Eisenhower's unheeded warning, the warning needed to be revived.

Not much came by post these days but this handsome square of vellum could have come no other way. Prabhakar drew out the card embossed with fine gold lettering. It was an invitation to Lisette's wedding. To nobility, it appeared. She had not told him the food entrepreneur she was going to marry was in the titled, privileged, nearly royal class, Lisette whom he had had the audacity to take through sweltering heat and meandering cows and buffalos to the kaif. But knowing himself he would have done so even had he known her background and lofty connections. And knowing Lisette, she had not mentioned, or had simply forgotten to, that her intended was kin to royalty because it had not occurred to her that this information was of any importance compared with the rapture of being in love. It was going to be a church wedding, Lisette ecstatic in bridal white, trailing a diaphanous veil, making vows to a man who Prabhakar hoped would be worthy of this exceptional woman, one who could surprise you with some new aspect of herself every five minutes.

There was a letter enclosed. She wrote, 'You must come, Prabhu, and bring a companion. We shall pay your fare and your wedding stay. We won't take no for an answer. It will be our gratitude to you for introducing me to the kaif. But for that visit we would not be opening our fabulous new restaurant.' Prabhakar was happy for her that she had seen fit to go ahead with her cherished plan and knowing Lisette, she would have found, somewhere on earth or a nearby planet, exactly the chef of her choice. The next para said: 'Please look at the gorgeous invitation to the opening of The Mughal which I designed. I've sent it to you by email. That's where we'll be having our wedding lunch party.'

Prabhakar did so and downloaded the invitation requesting the pleasure of his company. It was indeed special. Beautifully designed it was, as though on turquoise silk, and cunningly lettered to resemble Persian calligraphy. Lisette had attended to every detail with imagination and in her meticulous fashion. He scrolled further to the chef pictured on one side of the invitation—an unusual touch—elegantly attired in Mughal costume. Prabhakar was dumbfounded. He was looking at Rafeeq. This was Rafeeq elegantly attired, alive and well and prospering on Lisette's invitation. He enlarged the picture and there was no mistaking him.

He held his impatience and mounting irritation in check until late that evening when he rang Lisette.

'I know, I know, Prabhu, I do apologize but I couldn't tell you earlier. It was a question of secrecy, not knowing if he would be found and how to get him out if he was. Jimmy's uncle who's an absolute darling is the high commissioner in India and in all secrecy we appealed to him to consider the circumstances, explaining the danger Rafeeq was in after you told me what might happen to him. Jimmy's uncle was superb. He's dealt with these ghastly situations before and he has strong views. Don't ask me how they located Rafeeq but they did and kept him and his wife and two children on the official premises till their passports could be made and their passage arranged… Yes, I know, Prabhu, but as Rafeeq already had a job waiting for him here, and Jimmy's uncle had assured the authorities he was in the skilled category, there was no problem.'

The news was such a relief that Prabhakar found it hard to go on being angry with her for not telling him earlier and sparing him and Rahman their fears for Rafeeq's life and their own endless anxiety.

'Am I forgiven, Prabhu? Are we still friends? And you will come to the wedding and the opening, won't you?'

He said he had a better idea. A close friend of his, Rahman, who knew Rafeeq and his family much better than he did and had been in great distress about him, would be the perfect person to go, along with his wife. Lisette was disappointed but readily agreed.

'And there's another reason why I can't come, Lisette. I'm getting married too.'

Her small shriek of pure delight served as congratulation. But what about all the antecedents he didn't have? Prabhakar said Katerina had told him she had enough and to spare for both of them, including uncles and aunts. About to say more he condensed it for the hidden listener, saying the hey diddle diddle situation here needed his attention. Lisette was quick to understand. He put the phone down. Katerina sat across from him, waiting to resume their life together. The frightening mixture of joy and dread that the sight of her and the dangers of her work evoked, welled up in him. Love knows no safe haven in times like these. Yet Prahlad with his unerring instinct had given all lovers the only answer to that when he announced so jubilantly on that happiest of evenings: The times are grim, the times are unbearably tragic, and so, my friends—let's dance!

An Afterword to the Two Novels

HINDUS-IN-WONDERLAND

I wrote these two novels in an agony of mind to recreate in fiction what India was going through at the time of writing.

I was born and grew up when India was under British rule. During those years my family fought for freedom under the leadership of Mahatma Gandhi and my parents spent years of their lives in jail. My mother was imprisoned three times, my father four times, and he died in 1944 of his fourth imprisonment. He had fallen dangerously ill in Bareilly jail and was neither released for medical treatment in a hospital nor given any care or treatment in jail. No exception was made for a mortally ill political prisoner during that brutal wartime period. My uncle, Jawaharlal Nehru, with whom we shared his home, Anand Bhawan, in Allahabad, spent nearly ten years as a prisoner of the British government at different times in different jails.

In these harsh circumstances of growing up in a family committed to revolt against the occupying power, I became politically aware at an early age and when I began to write a few years after Independence, politics became the natural material of my writing, bringing alive not only the events, and through them the idealism and valour of India's unique non-violent fight for freedom, but also the events and atmosphere of independent India. Without my planning it, my novels became the story of the making of modern India.

Democracy—not religious rule—was the choice of government made by India's first Indian government, as was a celebration of our cultural and religious diversity by guaranteeing all Indians the right to live and worship as they chose.

There was admiration from abroad for a country struggling to overcome the impoverishment left by British rule through its plunder of India's wealth and resources, yet firmly resolved to revive and modernize itself without sacrificing individual rights and freedoms. When the Emergency of 1975–77 brought its shocking experience of dictatorship, it was Indian voters well-versed in their democratic rights who brought it down in a shattering electoral defeat.

The next major threat to the foundations of modern India came when the BJP was elected to power in 2014 with its mission of establishing a Hindu rashtra because it believes only Hindus are the rightful citizens of India. All others came as invaders and outsiders who have no right to claim citizenship. Since there is no territory on earth that has not at some time been invaded and occupied, nor denied citizenship on bogus grounds, this is fanciful thinking on the government's part, but we now live in a wonderland called Hindutva where wishful thinking prevails. Those who are called Others are under attack by the Hindutva brand of Hindus whom I call Hindus-in-Wonderland for the sheer fantasies they have set up as historical facts. Wonderlanders have invented the racial purity of Hindus before invasions polluted it by its mixture with invading races though there is no racially pure breed on earth, never has been and never will be.

For myself and millions of other Hindus, Hindus-in-Wonderland have nothing to do with Hinduism. Religious fanaticism was never a part of it. Now it rules the land and and we are watching the destruction of the secular democratic republic our founding fathers established, and which we have built on with pride since Independence.

My political awareness became painful as Hindus-in-Wonderland made it clear by their speeches and behaviour that violence was a virtue and violence against Others was perfectly all right. Fantasy extends to calling all opposition and all differences of opinion anti-national, anti-Indian, and by the peculiar new epithet: urban-Naxal. The men and women accused in this bizarre fashion—some of them known for their lifelong commitment to justice for tribals, the poor and unprivileged—are being persecuted in a variety of ways, including arrest on fake charges or no charges, imprisonment for years without trial in appalling conditions and savage treatment in jail.

In this environment of violence, vengance and lawlessness, where law is what Wonderland says it is, India's ancient and flourishing tradition of debate, discussion, disagreement and self-expression has been trashed, yet the over-arching fantasy of Hindus-in-Wonderland is that India is a democracy.

What can writers do in such times? They can write and the impulse to do so is overwhelming when the line between political and personal disappears and among the persecuted are friends and fellow-writers, artists, film-makers and activists dedicated to restoring democracy and human rights. So I had to write these two novellas one after the other, this time to bring alive the tragedy of the un-making of India.

NAYANTARA SAHGAL
Dehradun, February 2022